the
high-impact
infidelity
diet

MAIN

the
high-impact
infidelity
diet

a novel

lou harry and eric pfeffinger

THREE RIVERS PRESS
NEW YORK

Published in the United States by Three Rivers Press, an imprint of the Crown Publishing Group, a division of Random House, Inc., New York.
www.crownpublishing.com

Three Rivers Press and the Tugboat design are registered trademarks of Random House, Inc.

Library of Congress Cataloging-in-Publication Data
Harry, Lou, 1963–
   High-impact infidelity diet: a novel / Lou Harry & Eric Pfeffinger—
1st ed.
1. Overweight men—Fiction.   2. Reducing diets—Fiction.   3. Married
women—Fiction.   4. Weight loss—Fiction.   5. Prostitutes—Fiction.
6. Adultery—Fiction.   I. Pfeffinger, Eric.   II. Title.
   PS3608.A78386H54   2005
   813'.6—dc22   2005004667

ISBN 1-4000-9845-9

Printed in the United States of America

10 9 8 7 6 5 4 3 2 1

First Edition

For Larry & Stephanie, Marlene & Irv, and George & Kara: Three amazing, supportive, and sane couples who, while bearing absolutely no relation to the characters in this book, made its writing possible.

—lou

For everyone who said a book about dieting and hookers was a fantastic idea. You were both very supportive.

—eric

ACKNOWLEDGMENTS

This book would not be in your hands if it weren't for Robert Guinsler and Caroline Sincerbeaux. The authors also wish to thank early readers Eric Furman, Melissa Gregory, Cindy Harry, and the incredible shrinking Matt Wood for their time and suggestions. Finally, we are indebted to Little Debbie, Mrs. Butterworth, Big Boy, and Chef Boyardee—but, on some level, isn't everybody?

the
high-impact
infidelity
diet

BRIN

It's very simple, Martin. It really is.

But before I explain it, I want to point out that I just watched you sit on the porch eating an entire bag of Nutter Butters.

Do you know how much fat there is in one serving of Nutter Butters?

Do you know how many Nutter Butters there are in a serving?

I don't either. I'm sure it's somewhere around "lots and lots."

But that doesn't really matter. Well, it *does* matter, but it doesn't. The specifics don't matter. Well, they matter because they build up and they . . .

Let me start again. Because this is sounding like I'm nagging you and I don't want to nag you. Actually, I want to *stop* nagging you. That's what this is all about. It's just going to take five minutes. Ten, tops. Listen. All you have to do is listen. Sit down and listen.

It's not about trying. It's not about wanting to. You just *have* to lose weight. That's the fact here. You. Have. To.

I know: I told you this last year. Hell, I told you this every year we've been married. Remember the tux? I'm not going to bring it up again but you remember the tux. My mother mentioned the tux just last week. I told her not to bring it up. She brought it up. It's an embarrassing story no matter who brings it up.

But I don't want to embarrass you. This is not about that. I love you. I do.

You know that.

So here's the deal.

Take a look at this.

I know. It's from college. She went to my school. I'm not going to tell you her name.

Pretty, isn't she?

Well, she's even hotter now. I mean it. We're talking a very, very attractive woman. And she's your type. I know what type you like. When we were in Barbados I watched which women caught your attention. I know what you like. And she's it. She could be in Hollywood. She wanted to be but, well, she made some mistakes. I don't have to tell you her whole story. She's very happy now, though. And she makes good money.

Here's why I'm showing you this picture and why I'm going to tell you what I'm going to tell you: If anyone can keep you away from the Nutter Butters, it's somebody like her.

Don't say it. I know I'm attractive enough. I'm not putting myself down. I think I'm just fine for thirty-four and after two kids—okay, so they were from your first marriage—still, I've got nothing to apologize for. Plus you make me feel pretty. I do appreciate that.

Just shut up and listen. This isn't about me. It's about you. The guy I love. And the guy I want to have around for a good long time.

And it's about her. My friend from college. We met in film studies. Analyzing the male hierarchical gaze in American cinema. That sort of thing. Kind of ironic, actually, that she'd . . . well, I'm getting ahead of myself.

I know this is all confusing. I'm trying to tell you.

Okay, here's how it's going to be. Remember when we talked about free passes? You told me that, if the circumstances arose, I could spend the night with Christian Slater and if you had the opportunity, you could spend the night with Marie Osmond—you remember. We talked about it on the drive to Florida. It was late. We were getting silly. You tried to talk me into Donny. A surprising choice, Marie was, but that's why there's chocolate and vanilla. Of course, with Marie we're talking super double vanilla. Still, if that's what you want, that's cool. It's your free pass. Your free, boring, Mormon pass. I know, I shouldn't judge. It's not your fault you're a little bit country.

Sorry, back to the point.

I was thinking about it last week—not about the Osmonds, about the whole free pass thing. Our conversation on that drive kind of implied that there are certain cases—cases when it doesn't negatively impact our marriage—where it would be an okay thing if we have a, well, an encounter with someone. That was one case—or two cases, counting Donny—where a technical breach of vows wouldn't impact our marriage in any negative way. Well, if there's that case—those cases—I figured, maybe there's another. And maybe it doesn't have to be a celebrity and maybe . . .

No. No. No. No. No. Of course not, Martin. No. I didn't

want you to think that. No. This isn't anything like that. I haven't. Never. No. This is different. I know you're sensitive about . . . no. Just hear me out.

I talked with . . . well, I told you I don't want to give you her name right now. I talked with Her and I had heard that She had become a, well, a prostitute—a call girl, actually. It's not like She's stopping cars and wearing hot pants. There isn't a pimp involved or anything. It's just Her business. And after talking to Her for a while, I kind of had an idea.

No. No. No. No. Never. No. I'm not . . . Did you think I would . . . ? No. Yes, we could use some extra money considering your bonus situation last year but, no, that's not what I'm talking about. Just stop and shut up for a minute.

Here goes. Nutshell.

If you get down to 210 pounds, you sleep with her. One night.

No strings. No guilt. No last name. No hassle from me.

Because I want you around for a long time, and nothing else is working. Drop the weight and you get an unconditional night of fun with, seriously, the most beautiful woman I've ever met in my life.

I'll even drive you to the hotel and pick you up with a smile on my face the next morning.

I will. I mean that.

You need to wear a condom, of course. I should mention that now. I told her to insist. Nothing personal, but you never know how guys are going to be in situations like this. Not that I would imagine there are many situations like this. It's not like I got the idea out of *Reader's Digest*. It's not going to end up in "Life in These United States."

Nobody will know but me, you, and her.

And, well . . . Cheryl and Dierdre and I swore on our children, or lack thereof, that we would never tell anyone about this. Swore it. It was very Ya-Ya Sisterhood. I mean it. None of us are going to tell anyone. It would be like it happened in Vegas or something. Total secrecy on it. They're all cool with it.

Right now—we synchronized our watches—Cheryl and Dierdre are telling Doug and Randy exactly what I just told you. Well, maybe not exactly. There will be some natural differences in our presentational styles. For example, I haven't let you speak at all. Cheryl's probably not going to be able to do that with Doug.

Doug and Randy are going to get the same incentive that I just gave you, Martin. The same deal applies to them: Bring your weight under 210 and you get a night with my friend.

Seriously. Martin. If you think Jared had fun with Subway sandwiches, wait until you see what my friend can do.

MARTIN 316 POUNDS

I just stared at her.

I'm not sure for how long.

I just sat there not saying a word and letting her spin out this craziness. Like I was waiting for someone to stop her. Like there was going to be a phone call or someone knocking at the door or an anvil falling through the ceiling or something, anything, to change the scene, because when I came home from work there were very few things that I was expecting.

I expected to have to make dinner because I assumed that Brin would be working late. She usually works late on Tuesdays.

I also expected that the stink from the laundry room would be fierce because Philip, who is now ten and should be able to handle such things, was supposed to change the kitty litter last week and somehow never got around to it, although he found time to have instant message conversations with seven friends simultaneously for three hours last night. (I watched over his shoulder, then walked into the kitchen, poured a bowl of Froot Loops, and came back and he was still talking. Why didn't I stop him? Hell if I know. I guess I don't get to have him here that often so when he is here, I don't like to give him a hard time. Typical divorced parent behavior, maybe, but it works.)

I also expected that Regan, glorious Regan, would be dressed as some sort of witch princess and I'd have to rescue her or be rescued or whatever her five-year-old whim decided (it sometimes changes midstory, with whatever characters she's reading about at her mother's place sometimes working into the story and leaving me temporarily flummoxed).

And I expected to feel like a dad again, which is hard to do when your kids are living in Ohio with your ex-wife and her sister and her sister's kids like some sort of sitcom waiting to happen. (If it did happen, I'd be the guy who makes an appearance maybe once every twelve episodes.)

What I wasn't expecting was for my wife to tell me that I could have sex with a prostitute.

What I wasn't expecting was for her to reveal the fact that she even *knew* a prostitute.

In fact, I wasn't expecting prostitution in any shape or form to enter into our conversation. The last time we talked about prostitution was when we went to see that Jack the Ripper movie with Heather Graham and after the movie Brin said to me, "Before you met me, did you ever pay for it?"

I liked that she took it for granted that I didn't pay for it *since* I met her—which I haven't. I didn't beforehand either, although there was one time in Vegas when I made a call and checked prices. Show me a man who, alone in Vegas, hasn't called and checked prices and I'll show you the pope . . . who will probably tell you about the time he was in Vegas and he checked up on prices.

Still, I politely thanked the woman on the phone and hung up, satisfied—well, not quite satisfied—to fantasize about the whole prospect, assuming that the woman who knocked on the door would look like Julia Roberts or the one from *Leaving Las Vegas*. The actress who was in the babysitter movie and the one where Tom Cruise is the bartender. Not sure what happened to her. Probably will get a *CSI* show of her own one of these days.

The whole idea of paying for it—the whole idea of whores and call girls and prostitutes and whatever are a great wide world of "huh?" to me. Their world never intersected mine, as far as I could tell. If there was a whorehouse near Decatur, where I grew up, I didn't know about it. And it's not like any of my friends ever reported back to me on experiences with prostitutes. Hookers are like astronauts. I know they exist. I know they do amazing things. But it's just outside of my experience. Is their price structure based on time or activity? Is it cheaper to go to a whorehouse or have them come to your hotel room? Can you suggest how they dress? Are they . . .

See, that's what happens. I don't think about it. She mentions it. And suddenly the window is open in the middle of a storm and all kinds of shit is blowing into my mind.

Focus, I said to myself while she was spilling out this scheme. Once I got what she was talking about and once I was convinced that she wasn't pulling my leg—that this wasn't some sicko reality show—the first thing I wanted to do was call Doug and Randy.

The second thing I wanted to do was *not* call Doug and Randy.

Yes, they are my friends.

No, we don't talk about sex. Not real sex anyway. We talk about hotties and we tell jokes and we weigh the relative appeal of Eurobreasts versus good old American augmentation balloons and we talk about rumors, about people at our respective places of employment, about whoever is on the *Sports Illustrated* swimsuit issue cover, about whatever. But we've got kind of an unwritten law that I didn't think about until about now.

That law is this: We don't talk about our own sex lives.

Honestly, I don't know if Doug and Randy are doing it with their wives on a daily basis or if they haven't done it since Y2K (I'm pretty sure we *all* did it on Y2K—just in case it was our last shot before the world monetary system collapsed). (Or maybe that was just me.)

All this was spinning through my mind. My mind was working overtime on this. Like it was doing high-level calculus. But to Brin, all I was doing was sitting there.

Staring.

Until she said, "Well, that's the offer. I won't bring it up again. I'm not even going to ask you whether you want to do it or not because then you might feel like there's some judgment on you when you agree or when you say no. Instead, I'm telling you. You are doing this. You're going to lose the weight. You're going to look like the you I've only seen in pictures. You're going to spend the night with her. No discussion. No negotiation. Let me know

when you're ready to check the scale. I've already calibrated the one in the upstairs bathroom."

And she left.

And the word *calibrated* reverberated in my brain.

I don't think I've ever heard her use the word *calibrated*. And here she's telling me that she calibrated, all
premeditated, the upstairs scale—which I haven't
stepped on in a decade. How much of this speech had
she rehearsed? Did she and Cheryl and Dierdre practice
this thing, pick a secretary, write it out and make copies?
Is there any documentation?

None of that is important, of course, but those details
are easier to think about, easier to wrap my mind around,
than the basic concept of this screwed-up offer.

My wife is giving me permission to sleep with another woman.

Not a never-gonna-happen free pass with a celebrity
I'll never meet (although I thought I saw Marie Osmond
at the outlet mall once, from a distance, over by Eddie
Bauer).

Not an I-don't-mind-if-you-want-to-turn-on-*Monster's
Ball*-for-the-Halle-Berry-sex-scene-while-we're-having-
sex offer.

This is a full-fledged have-an-all-night-party-with-
another-woman-no-strings-attached offer. No, not offer,
demand.

She wants me to do this.

She is making me do this. Not giving me a choice.

What I should be doing is dancing around the room. I
should have thrown my arms around her and kissed her

and maybe made love with her right there on the couch. (We did that once, three years ago. I scraped a knee.)

That's what I should have done. Because, come on, it's an amazing offer. Deal. Whatever. It qualifies me for luckiest fat guy of the decade. I should get an award at a ceremony, a statuette—the gold-hardened artery, handed to me by Drew Carey and Harvey Weinstein, Karl Rove is in the audience applauding, he just won the William Howard Taft Award for Most Powerful Fat Sonofabitch, it's an annual ceremony where the lifetime achievement awards are given out before age thirty-nine because anything later is just pushing everyone's luck. . . .

Okay. Focus.

Fact is, I was a little too shocked by the whole thing to do much of anything. When I finally found her again in the house, it was like nothing had been said. We ate (I didn't get seconds). We watched some TV. I put the kids to bed. I felt like taking a shower, so I did.

And I waited until she was asleep before I did it. I could have just locked the door, of course, or done it while she was downstairs, but instead I waited until she was letting out that soft snore and I climbed out of bed and walked back to the bathroom.

Yes, it was calibrated. The needle pointed straight at the zero. It was also cleaned. It looked like she had scrubbed the thing. I never realized it was dirty.

Not looking down at the scale meant looking straight ahead at the mirror.

The guy who looked back at me was, well, large.

Very large.

Larger than he's ever been in his life. Larger than his father—who once smacked him for using the term "fatty" to describe his sister. Larger than TV detective Frank Cannon (Who the hell played him? Not Raymond Burr, that was Ironside, the one in the wheelchair . . .). Larger than "before" pictures in before-and-after ads.

A fat guy.

But that was no surprise. I knew I had become a fat guy. It would take denial more powerful than da Nile to not know that.

I looked down. I had to kind of maneuver so that I could see that the fat guy weighed 316 pounds.

To: Doug@linklink.com, MBB@yahoo.com
From: Randy12479@aol.com
Subject: Quick questions

1. Do either of you know anyone who fixes gutters?
2. What about that Bears game last night?
3. Did you guys have the same really, really bizarre conversation last night with Cheryl and Brin that I had with Dierdre?

—Randy Tonelli

"Football is like nuclear warfare. There are no winners, just survivors."—Frank Gifford.

To: Randy12479@aol.com, Doug@linklink.com
From: MBB@yahoo.com
Subject: This thing

Yep.

—Martin

To: Randy12479@aol.com, MBB@yahoo.com
From: Doug@linklink.com
Subject: This thing

Yeah. Brin's sorority must have had some fucking kick-ass parties.

—Doug

Doug E. Garrison, Sales Manager
T.H.E. Solutions, "Better people through business"
One Park Plaza

This e-mail is the property of T.H.E. Solutions and is subject to scrutiny accordingly. This account is strictly for professional use only.

To: Randy12479@aol.com, Doug@linklink.com
From: MBB@yahoo.com
Subject: This thing

And a very busy treasurer.

—Martin

To: Randy12479@aol.com, MBB@yahoo.com
From: Doug@linklink.com
Subject: This thing

So, what, are we going to do it?

—Doug

Doug E. Garrison, Sales Manager
T.H.E. Solutions, "Better people through business"
One Park Plaza

***This e-mail is the property of T.H.E. Solutions and is subject
to scrutiny accordingly. This account is strictly for professional
use only.***

DOUG 307 POUNDS

I'm hypnotized by my man breasts. I never even realized I had man breasts before. Not until that fucked-up conversation with Cheryl.

Not that she uttered the words *Doug, you have man breasts,* though she could have. Would have been valid, because, well, I demonstrably do. But after said fucked-up conversation I come into the bathroom to get some perspective, take a long hard look, see what the goddamn fuss is about, and whoop, there they are, in the mirror, shocking, scary, like movie monsters: man breasts. *The Man Breasts That Ate Miami. Frankenstein and the Wolf-Man Meet the Man Breasts.*

So now I'm spending quality time with my man breasts. Hello, man breasts.

Man breasts is one of those phrases that sounds funny the more you say it. Man breasts. Man breasts. Man breasts. Man breasts. Man breasts. Man breasts. Man breasts. Man breasts. Man breasts. Man breasts. Man breasts. Man breasts. Man breasts.

Actually, it's really not. It starts out kind of funny and then gets less funny the more you say it.

Quart—that's a word that gets funnier. Quart. Quart. Quart. Quart. Quart. See?

Fuck. Shit. Is it possible these things could really kill me? Cheryl thinks they will. She thinks my vital, dynamic life force could get snuffed out under the cushy, blobby, harmless, comforting weight of these homicidal man breasts. Remington Steele would come in, find me dead, and pepper the man breasts with pointed questions. Andy Sipowicz would sternly warn the man breasts not to leave town.

That chick on *Remington Steele,* she was hot.

So was Cheryl, when we met. I'm not saying she isn't now. She probably is. I suppose there are guys who think she's as hot now as I thought she was then. Who am I to say? Of course, she was dating Matt, a fraternity brother of mine when I met her, so how the Christ was I supposed to not fall for her? I was a little disappointed, okay, when Matt didn't get mad when I slept with her. He acted relieved, actually. "I was thinking of dumping her," he says. "She's too mouthy." At first I thought he said "mousy," and my temper actually flared (which surprised me, I'd fucked this girl, what, once?) and I shoved the asshole and I said, "She's not mousy. Her chest is too big to be mousy, for one."

No, he goes, "mouthy. She's mouthy." Okay, that I had to concede. In fact, a big reason I stayed with her beyond a couple weeks was because the way she'd take the piss out of my frat brothers at parties and meals was funny as shit. They hated her, but that was a plus, too—it was senior year and I was getting sick as fuck of those guys.

The way she'd take the piss out of me was less funny but still kind of amusing.

For a while.

Fuck you, man breasts. And fuck you for suddenly

being noticeable after this crazy talk with Cheryl. I mean, you've been with me for a long time, right? Since college, right? When I first started going with Cheryl she went on and on about how she didn't usually like frat guys but that I was different from the other guys in my fraternity and I said "How am I different?" and she said "Well, you're fatter, for one." So you two have been a part of this marriage from the beginning. I've showered with you. Trapped tossed footballs against you. Squeezed women against you. Why the hell didn't I notice you and your hypnotic powers before?

But know this, man breasts: I'm too strong to be taken down by the likes of you. I'm not some 305-pound (plus or minus) weakling. See that guy in the mirror? Those unblinking nips are staring back at a guy who has survived his share of shit. My dad dying when I was twelve, for one. Then I got shingles. Uh, that IRS audit. I've been through too much. And frankly, I don't know what the problem is. Are they so unattractive? Really?

I mean, yes, sure, I know they are. They're unattractive by definition. Women don't see me go by and say "Check out that dude's rack." They're two large, two distinctive, exotic natural land formations. Only words from Randy's fucking word-a-day vocabulary-building self-improvement calendar could appropriately describe these fuckers. Pendulous. Hirsute. Wagnerian. Uh. Mnemonic.

(Never apologized to Randy for that day, when, in front of his kid, I said I was going to take the word-a-day calendar and shove it up his cloaca. He's been distant since. Martin says I'm too insensitive. Fuck them.)

It's not like they repel women. They've never once caused a woman to scream and clutch her head. It's not like I take off my shirt and there's the phantom of the fucking opera. Can't tell Cheryl that. "The other women I've slept with since we got married—all twenty-three of them, twenty-four if you count that one where I'm not sure what the fuck happened—don't seem to mind." "Oh, okay."

Curse you, man breasts. I curse you and the mozzarella sticks that spawned you.

To hell with you both.

I do my best to ignore you, let you thrive through my benign neglect, and this is how you repay me? By causing long serious conversations with my wife? Is this a friendly thing to do?

(Well, as serious as a conversation with my wife can be, considering she kept referring to the prostitute as "Sexy McHumpsalot." That did tend to undermine the gravitas.)

Still: deep discussions after work about commitment and mortality and saturated fats? Fuck fuck fuck fuck you, man breasts.

"Fuck," not so funny over and over.

When I move vigorously, they sway in unison. Graceful. Elegant. Like two synchronized swimmers.

Maybe I should name them. You're Stan, and you on the left will be Esther. Or. No. Koko.

If it weren't for you, man breasts, my loving wife, Cheryl, wouldn't be beseeching me to complete a series of feats that will allow me to sleep with another woman. Someone Brin went to school with? A pro? The woman's cute as hell, with dimples. Hot. Nice-looking.

Thank you, man breasts.

But fuck, I don't really want to sleep with her.

I mean, of course I want to sleep with her, but I don't like the circumstances. Don't like them at all. Don't like Cheryl controlling my sex life. Worse, I don't like Dierdre and Brin contributing to the control of my sex life. Wrong in a thousand ways. Jesus, that's wrong.

Of course the very thought of missing out on this opportunity is supposed to kill me. The thought of the whole thing is supposed to drive me to Jack LaLanne Land with the weight flying off while I pursue this great prize. The screwed-up thing is—well, one of the screwed-up things is—I'm sure I'm alone in wishing this deal never hit the table.

Randy will be up for it. No doubt about that. If Dierdre helped hatch the plan, then in his henpecked little heart, it has to be good.

Martin will buy in, too, because . . . I don't know why. I'm not a fucking psychologist. But he will. No question about it.

Me, I've got a more complicated situation, the crux of which is this: How the fuck am I supposed to treat this like it's a one-of-a-kind, once-in-a-lifetime opportunity to transcend my marriage vows when I can get tail every time I go on the road? Well, almost every time. I'm batting about .60. Nice tail, too, although, you know, sometimes you combine conventioneer standards with beer goggles and you come up with something semifrightening.

But semifrightening without strings isn't so bad when you're in Detroit. Or Springfield. Or Knoxville.

So I'm good.

Life is fine.

I don't need this.

But Cheryl doesn't know that. Which means, unlike the other guys, I have no fucking choice in the matter. I'm basically being forced into diet and exercise.

Because if I don't, if I go "Thanks but no thanks, hon, that's sweet," Cheryl will know something's up. She'll know either I'm gay or I've been unfaithful. And because she's seen me with the Anna Kournikova calendar at Barnes & Noble, she'll know I've been unfaithful.

And then you, man breasts, are the least of my problems.

So I have to lose weight.

And then I have to sleep with this woman my wife's best friend picked out.

And I have to pretend to be excited about the whole thing.

And I'll be sleeping with a woman—with my wife's endorsement—with the full knowledge of Martin and Randy and their wives, which means that pretty much the only way this could get any less arousing is if they figured out some way to get my mother and Madeleine Albright involved.

I blame you for this, Stan. Koko. This is entirely your fucking fault.

Well, I guess it's also sort of my fault for the cheating. But I'd rather blame you. Both of you. Look at me when I'm talking to you! Yeah, that's right: You better quiver.

RANDY 303 POUNDS

Pro/Con List

PRO: Losing weight is healthy. Fat people get heart attacks.
CON: People also get heart attacks while exercising.

PRO: It would send a good message to Ty.
CON: Ty is a preteen. They don't understand messages.

PRO: I used to feel really good when I was in shape. It would be good to feel good like that.
CON: I don't feel that bad now. Honest. I really don't.

PRO: Of course, it would be good to have more stamina.
CON: I really like fudge-covered Oreos, more than I thought I ever could like anything (besides Dierdre, and God and stuff).

PRO: If I lose weight, I get to have sex with that friend of Brin's.
CON: Do I really want to have sex with that friend of Brin's?

PRO: Yeah, of course I do. I mean, I'm a straight guy and she's really attractive.
CON: I'm pretty sure having sex with someone besides Dierdre is wrong.

PRO: Except that Dierdre is saying I can do it.
CON: She's kind of making me do it.

PRO: Then why does it feel so wrong?
CON: Maybe that's how you know it will feel so good.

PRO: I think I've lost the point of this pro/con list.
CON: Yeah, this list isn't working. Not at all. It would be nice if it did. Then I could give a certain weight to each of the pros and each of the cons and, once I exhaust the topic, add them up and see which one wins. It sounded like a really good idea when the therapist on TV recommended the pro/con list, as a good way to deal with a decision or a crisis.

Now that I think about it, I'm not sure if he's a therapist on TV or one of those people who plays a therapist on TV. Same diff probably.

I should have watched to see if he said exactly how to do the pro/con list. Now that I've tried one for myself, well, it's not as easy as I thought it was. Plus I wonder if I should be using graph paper, and where do you buy graph paper these days?

Maybe I just shouldn't be worrying so much about it. I bet Martin and Doug aren't worrying so much. I bet they're all like, "Yeah!"

But their marriages are really strong.

Of course, *my* marriage is really strong. Really, really strong.

I can make that a Pro. Like this:

PRO: My marriage is really, really strong.

CON: Lots of marriages are strong. But it probably only takes one thing, like one big thing, to change that. A big thing like, oh, I don't know, maybe sleeping with someone else. That can make a strong marriage go from strong to, like, pendulous.

Still, Dierdre says it's okay. Ooh, ooh, there's another one.

PRO: Dierdre says it's okay.

CON: But does that make it okay?

PRO: It probably does. And what does what anyone else says matter in this situation?

CON: I'm losing control of the list again.

PRO: Get a hold of yourself.

Well, huh. Okay. So, on this list anyway, the pros outnumber the cons, so that's got to mean something. Maybe Dierdre's right. Maybe this will be good for everyone.

And that woman really is hot, although maybe it would be easier to say yes if she wasn't. If she was just, well, average and I knew that I wouldn't compare her to Dierdre—I would just enjoy her as someone different, not as someone potentially better. In just looks, I mean. Dierdre is, well, she's great. Really great. The best. So there's no threat to anything here. No risk of anything.

And Dierdre said she thought Brin remembered that this woman was really smart, which makes things . . . I don't know what that makes things. Kind of intimidating, maybe. So . . .

So.

I feel like I should have negotiated. Like, haggled. Over the terms. Gotten her up to 220 pounds, maybe. What if the other guys negotiated? It's like being the only guy on the car lot paying sticker price. I've been there. Don't like it.

CON: I should have negotiated.
PRO: The woman's really smart. So.

CON: So.

To: Doug@linklink.com, MBB@yahoo.com
From: Randy12479@aol.com
Subject: Dumb question

Did you guys negotiate? Strike a better deal than 210 pounds?

—Randy

"Victory is all about attention to detale."

To: Randy12479@aol.com, Doug@linklink.com
From: MBB@yahoo.com
Subject: RE: Dumb question

Randy, it's not a Turkish bazaar.

—Martin

To: Randy12479@aol.com, MBB@yahoo.com
From: Doug@linklink.com
Subject: RE: Dumb question

Yeah, Randy. I negotiated. Got her up to 214 pounds and in exchange I promised not to enjoy my orgasm that much.
  Dumbass.

—Doug

Doug E. Garrison, Sales Manager
T.H.E. Solutions, "Better people through business"
One Park Plaza

This e-mail is the property of T.H.E. Solutions and is subject to scrutiny accordingly. This account is strictly for professional use only.

To: Doug@linklink.com, MBB@yahoo.com
From: Randy12479@aol.com
Subject: RE: RE: Dumb question

No need to be gross, man.

—Randy

"It's always darkest before the dawn."

MARTIN 315 POUNDS

Robert Conrad. That was the guy who played Cannon on TV. Robert Conrad.

Or maybe it was William Conrad. Something like that.

Conrad Bain?

DOUG 307 POUNDS

How big is Doug?
   Sooooo big.
   So fucking big.
   But not as big as Martin.

RANDY 303 POUNDS

Dierdre gave Ty and his friend Rich a pair of my pants so that they could go out trick-or-treating as Chang and Eng.
I hate Halloween.

To: Doug@linklink.com, MBB@yahoo.com
From: Randy12479@aol.com
Subject: Doing it or not doing it

I think it's the kind of thing where we should all do it or none of us should do it because here's why:

   1. If one of us does it but not the rest, that person will feel like a jerk.
   1.a. Unless it's you, Doug.
   2. If two of us do it and one doesn't, that person will feel like a loser.

   This all, of course, assumes that we actually reach the goal. Have either of you talked with a doctor or anybody about whether this is a healthy thing to do? I mean, it's not like they gave us a time limit or anything but still . . .

—Randy

"Losing is for losers."

To: BrinM@compumail.net
From: Chercher@worknet.com
Subject: RE: The Plan

Brin-ster,
Talked to Doug. He's into it. But we knew he would be. I
might have gotten the same results by saying that if he
dropped to 210 pounds he could have ten minutes alone
with a picture of Soledad O'Brien. I'm guessing he gets
down to 255 max (or is it min?) without my having to say another word about it. Why don't I think of these things?
Maybe because I lack your capacity for evil, I mean genius.

Loveyameanit,
C.

To: BrinM@compumail.net
From: Chercher@worknet.com
Subject: Oh, and a few other things . . .

Also: Remember you promised to show me how to calibrate
a scale.
  Remember you promised to go out with me to buy a scale.
  Remember you promised to lend me a tranquilizer gun so
Doug wouldn't run screaming from the very sight of a scale.
  Remember you promised to give me some engineering dia-
grams I could use to explain to Doug exactly what is a scale.

Remember you promised to give me empty consoling phrases to use to console Doug when he gets on the scale and it has to report his weight in scientific notation.

Remember you promised to go with me to have my head examined after this all goes horribly terribly wrong. j/k. I know it will work exactly as well as you said it will, and not work exactly as well as you promised it won't.

Loveyameanit,

C.

RANDY 303 POUNDS

Brilliant idea. Proud of myself, I must say.

I took the Halloween candy—the deliberate leftovers that I kept in the plastic cauldron in the garage and dip into whenever, well, whenever I'm in the garage—and filled about fifteen paper bags. Then, this morning, I left them on doorsteps up and down the block.

What the heck. Create a holiday. Former Fat Guys' Day.

MARTIN 315 POUNDS

This afternoon, at lunch, I had applesauce instead of fries as the side dish.

The battle begins.

BRIN

I knew you'd be onboard for this, Cheryl. But Dierdre I didn't know about—I guess I never know about Dierdre really. You've known her longer than I have, so—okay, maybe Dierdre is inherently unknowable. Ineffable. Like the will of God, only blonder.

Or maybe we're just trying to read in too much. Maybe trying to figure her out is like taking a graduate course in *Saved by the Bell.* Just an intellectual exercise with nothing really to gain.

Actually, since Dierdre's pretty much responsible for my meeting Martin, I should cut her some slack. You knew that. No, you did, remember? Martin was divorced and all lonely and pathetic, I'm told, and Dierdre found out that the building where she was taking her acting and batik lessons also was holding one of those speed-dating sessions so she told him he should go? And he went, reluctantly and full of shame? And in the hallway outside the room with the speed-dating session he ran into me, and he assumed I was there for the speed-dating session and he said he really didn't want to do that, why didn't we go out instead and get some coffee, so we did?

I never told him that I wasn't there for the speed-dating session, that I had just stopped on my way home from work to look for a pay phone to order some Thai, and that if you'd asked me ten minutes earlier I would have said I'd never marry a guy who even considered attending a speed-dating session. But here I am, and here we are.

Do I sound like I don't like Dierdre? I do. How could you not? It would be like not liking kittens. Except I don't like kittens. Still—flaw in my character. Not in hers. Remind me next time we're together to say something nice about Dierdre. Not fake nice. Nice nice.

To: Doug@linklink.com, MBB@yahoo.com
From: Randy12479@aol.com
Subject: The Challenge

Just thought you'd like to know: I'm down two pounds.
  Eat my dust.

—Randy

"Give me victory or give me death."

To: Randy12479@aol.com
CC: MBB@yahoo.com
From: Doug@linklink.com
Subject: Your dust

Randy, you lose two pounds when you clip your fingernails.

—Doug

Doug E. Garrison, Sales Manager
T.H.E. Solutions, "Better people through business"
One Park Plaza

This e-mail is the property of T.H.E. Solutions and is subject to scrutiny accordingly. This account is strictly for professional use only.

To: Randy12479@aol.com
CC: Doug@linklink.com
From: MBB@yahoo.com
Subject: Your dust

Randy, you lose two pounds when you blow your nose.

—Martin

To: MBB@yahoo.com
From: Doug@linklink.com
Subject: Your dust

Martin, give it up. I beat you—with basically the same joke—by four minutes. As a consolation prize, check out this: www.hottiehottiehottie.com/index/411/large

—Doug

Doug E. Garrison, Sales Manager
T.H.E. Solutions, "Better people through business"
One Park Plaza

This e-mail is the property of T.H.E. Solutions and is subject to scrutiny accordingly. This account is strictly for professional use only.

To: Doug@linklink.com
From: MBB@yahoo.com
Subject: The hottiehottiehottie

Please don't tell me that you devoted a portion of your hard drive to that particular honey (and I mean "honey" in the Winnie-the-Pooh's-fat-ass-stuck-in-the-door sense). If you did, I'm surprised you had room for anything else.

—Martin

To: MBB@yahoo.com
From: Doug@linklink.com
Subject: The hottiehottiehottie

How do you know she's not the prize? That was an old picture we were shown.

  Besides, with her we could all take care of business at once and probably wouldn't even run into each other.

—Doug

Doug E. Garrison, Sales Manager
T.H.E. Solutions, "Better people through business"
One Park Plaza

This e-mail is the property of T.H.E. Solutions and is subject to scrutiny accordingly. This account is strictly for professional use only.

To: Doug@linklink.com
From: MBB@yahoo.com
Subject: The hottiehottiehottie

I'll say it right now. If we all get to that magic number, I'm either going first or I want her thoroughly disinfected after you do your business.

Maybe even sandblasted.

Even then, I'm waiting at least a week for her to air out.

—Martin

To: MBB@yahoo.com
From: Doug@linklink.com
Subject: The hottiehottiehottie

What makes you think I'll be done with her in a week?

—Doug

Doug E. Garrison, Sales Manager
T.H.E. Solutions, "Better people through business"
One Park Plaza

This e-mail is the property of T.H.E. Solutions and is subject to scrutiny accordingly. This account is strictly for professional use only.

To: Doug@linklink.com
From: MBB@yahoo.com
Subject: The hottiehottiehottie

Better question: What makes me think she'll be done with her penicillin in a week?

—Martin

To: Doug@linklink.com
From: Randy 12479@aol.com
Subject: Two pounds

Oh yeah? Well, you'll lose two pounds if you'd just clean out your belly button.

—Randy

"A miss is as good as a mile."

To: Randy12479@aol.com
From: Doug@linklink.com
Subject: Two pounds

Nice one, Randy.

BRIN

Thanks for being my morning-walk buddy, Cheryl. I've walked this neighborhood so many times I think I'd lose my mind with boredom if I didn't have company. And I can't exactly afford to stop exercising now, can I, not after what we've asked the guys to do. I've officially forfeited my god-given right as a monogamous married person to Let Myself Go. We both have. Pretty much in perpetuity. Geez. What kind of idiots are we?

Yeah, I thought about asking Dierdre to come along, but she's not within walking distance, and I still harbor this instinctive resistance to the idea of anyone driving somewhere in order to walk. It's a vestigial but still palpable part of my animal brain, left over from back before our species evolved into suburbanites. Plus she doesn't work, she just has all those classes, which means she can walk any time she wants to, and I don't know why that makes a difference to me but it does. For the record, when I had lunch with Dierdre on Tuesday I did tell her that I liked her shoes. And I tried to laugh when she laughed at things that weren't particularly funny. So I'm making the effort. Points for me. And they were good shoes.

But I really don't want to walk with her. Dierdre is fast, and she looks better than I do so I'm self-conscious. Much more comfortable with you.

Hey, no spitting at your walking buddy!

So here's where I am on this. Bear with me. There's Nicole Vinicor's house. She has credit cards her husband doesn't even know about. Marjorie Yurgin? When she has sex with Mike she secretly fantasizes about—get this— her sex toys. Neil Wimbush has no idea that Leanne was married twice before.

What's my point? My point is, everyone in this neighborhood lies to their beloved spouses. Difference is, we're lying for their own good. Not to avoid confrontation, or to ensure our own pleasure or comfort, or to gain materially. We're lying to our husbands for their health and well-being. We invented an old prostitute friend with an expensive B.A. degree in the interest of virtue, selflessness, and public health. Someone should give us a medal, really. And as long as they never make it down to 210 pounds—and let's be real, that ain't gonna happen—no one ever needs to find out that we're lying rotten bitches.

Yes, very good. You see now that my morning walks are less about aerobic cardio and more about exercising my capacity for self-delusional rationalization.

It's terribly healthy. Hard as a rock.

I have Denial of Steel. Buy my exercise tapes.

RANDY 301 POUNDS

Middle of the night, here's what Dierdre says to me:

"It's not that I don't love you exactly the way you are. I do. You know that. You're my prince. But you know that, too. You know I'm yours until the end of time. And since you know these things then maybe you aren't that motivated to do this thing that would be really healthy for you and make our time together even longer. I get really scared sometimes like when you were shoveling snow and I watched out the window and saw you leaning on the shovel just staring at nothing when you were only out there five minutes.

"And I'll tell you right now that I never lied to you except that I didn't tell you that I called next door and asked the Barringtons to send their son over to shovel for you and I told him to tell you he was doing it as a class project in good deeds, but really I paid him twenty bucks, but that's the only thing I lied about and I only lied about it because I knew you wouldn't pay him and I didn't want the ambulance to have to come for you on roads as icy as they were that day."

The plows never do come into our neighborhood. The city roads could be clear for a week and it's still like the Ice Follies in our development. I talked to the Community Council about it back when I used to go to Community

Council meetings to improve both my community and my public speaking skills. They made a note of it.

"What I'm saying," she said, "is that this is okay. It really is. I love you. You love me . . ."

"Barney the dinosaur loves both of us."

"Funny." She didn't really think it was that funny. "We love each other and I think this is fun and good and cool and I know you are going to make it. And it's going to be our secret. Just the six of us."

"What about the priest?"

"What priest?"

"Don't I have to confess this?"

"Oh."

"You know, I think you're going to have to confess it, too."

"You think so?"

"Of course."

"But what sin am *I* committing?"

"So you think it's a sin if I do stuff with her? Then why are you . . . ?"

"We've done a bunch of sins together, right. Remember that time up at the Dunes?"

"But do you think this is really a sin? If you give me permission?"

"I don't know. When it's done," she said, "you'll ask the priest in confession. You can go to another parish if you want. I did that once in high school."

"You what?"

"Not important. You'll confess it and it'll be done. What's the priest going to do, not forgive you? It's his job.

I'm sure he's heard a lot worse . . . not that this is bad . . . or even a sin, maybe." We looked at the ceiling a little while. "Did I tell you Brin said she liked my shoes? Brin's so sweet."

"I probably should've known, huh?"

"What?"

"The Barrington kid, shoveling our snow. Who takes a class in good deeds?"

"Yeah."

"But I didn't know. Who knows, you know? What kids are learning in school these days?"

"I had a feeling you sort of knew, without knowing you knew," she said. "You're always smarter than your brain thinks you are."

"Yeah?"

"You're my big smart Einstein brain."

"That's me."

MARTIN 315 POUNDS

We were in the kitchen.

I was getting a beer for Brin while Doug was searching for something in the refrigerator—some kind of new mayonnaise spread or something. He buys crap like that. All the time. Like regular mayonnaise or ketchup or whatever isn't good enough. If it's been messed with by some think-tank test-lab white suits somewhere, Doug's got to try it.

I swear Cheryl has never seen the inside of a supermarket. She's great with car repairs, hanging pictures, double entendres, all that stuff, but Doug does all the grocery shopping. I've been on the way home from Pibb's Bar with him—back when we used to go to Pibb's more often—and he'd say, "I just need to run in for some milk. I promised Cheryl I'd bring home a gallon of milk" and I'd wait in the car and he'd come out with three bags of groceries including combo peanut butter/jelly spread or some peach salsa shit.

(Can't make fun of him for it, either. That's one of several things about Doug that you learn you better not make fun of, like his weapons-grade aftershave or his comic books. He'll get all pouty and the fun will be over. Makes one wonder why he married a woman who makes fun of, like, everything.)

"So this is the way it's going to be," I said at the refrigerator. "Are we just not going to talk about it when we're all together? E-mail is fine but no talking about it. Is that the rule?"

"I don't know," he said, head inside the fridge. "Nobody gave me a rule book."

"I figured we'd talk about it. Not that I want to talk about it. It feels kind of weird to talk about it with Brin and Cheryl. . . ."

"But we're not talking about it. . . ."

"I know."

"Then why does it feel weird?"

I wasn't sure. Sometimes I don't remember exactly what I say and then when I get questioned on it, I freeze up. Even with friends. So I decided to start again from another direction.

"It's just that this is the first time we've all been together," I said, "since the thing was brought up."

"Is that what we're calling it? 'The thing'?" Doug said.

"I don't give a shit what we call it. . . ."

"We've got to call it something. 'The thing' seems kind of science fictiony. I don't like it."

"You got something better to call it?"

"Like it's going to come popping out from behind a crashed spaceship or something."

"So what do you want to call it?"

"I don't know," Doug said. " 'The deal,' maybe. Or 'The goal.' "

"The prize."

"The accomplishment."

"The situation."

"The Bizarro-world freaky shit."

"The . . . uh . . . situation?"

"The fucking nightmare of a headache. Where the fuck is my red pepper aioli?"

And then Cheryl came in with some appetizer plates and started shoveling leftovers into the disposal—there were lots of leftovers. I know I only had a bite or two of the brown pasta thing. I don't think Doug or Randy had much more. And I know Brin doesn't like chicken wings.

So it was obvious to everyone that we weren't eating much, at least not in front of each other. So there was that, too. Not only were we not going to talk about "the thing" or "the deal" or whatever the hell, but we also weren't going to eat much while in each other's company.

This is going to suck.

Because we used to talk a lot about food, and we used to joke a lot about sex. From here on out, though, it looked like there would be no nudge-nudge, wink-wink jokes. No wiseass remarks. And no scarfing down pizzas while watching games on TV. As a social entity, we'll exist like nothing has happened except the three guys have decided to drop some pounds. But, man, it's going to be different than before. What are we supposed to talk about? Books?

Last night, I dreamed about the girl in the picture. She was on an island. I was wearing a big sombrero and carrying a box of Tinkertoys.

Dreams are bullshit.

RANDY 301 POUNDS

Martin and I met fifteen years ago, when he was still married to Amy. Martin knew Doug since they were kids. When Doug moved back here from Texas, we all started hanging out. So I guess the guys are the center of this friendship. But if you ask our wives, they'll tell you that they are the core.

I won't argue. Nothing to argue about.

Because they're kind of right. See, Dierdre and Brin and Cheryl share stuff with each other. They tell each other what they are feeling and what they are thinking. Amy used to be part of the group and it's sort of weird but good, I guess, that Brin has slipped right in, like Amy was never there, like she's been running the Randy-Martin-Doug Ladies' Auxiliary forever.

Whenever I see the three of them together I can feel the shared secrets pouring off them like a bad perfume. They go to lunch together. They have their once-a-month movie club together. They share books until they don't even know who bought what.

Doug, Martin, and I sometimes go to a ball game. Or we go out for a beer. Or we go bowling. If I suggested we share books, they'd look at me like an alien took over my brain. I'm not that into books anyway. Apart from ones about aliens who take over brains.

I don't think I've ever told Martin anything important.

Never cracked any life secrets. Haven't shared a whole lot with Doug, either. And neither of them has told me anything important, either. Martin didn't even say much when he and Amy split. "We're going through some shit," he said and the next thing we knew, he was saying that she's moving out and saying that she's taking the kids and saying that they're heading for Ohio. I meant to tell Martin that if he needed to talk he could just call me but I don't think I did. Never came up.

There were exactly three times when I considered talking to Doug and/or Martin about anything important.

1. When it looked like the new boss at my old job was going to clean house and I was the canary in the coal mine. Martin and I were out for a beer and I was going to tell him how terrifying it was to try to put together a résumé after fifteen years at one place, not even knowing anything about, like, fonts.

2. When Dierdre was convinced Doug was cheating on Cheryl and wanted me to narc on him. That was at 11:30 one night and I considered talking to him about it, not sure if I would report back anything to Dierdre or not. The next night, at about 11:30 again, she apologized and told me that she had put me in a really difficult position and I shouldn't have to choose between loyalty to my friends and loyalty to my wife and so I didn't have to tell her anything. Like with bachelor parties. Or the CIA.

3. When I was getting those pains in my chest and I thought for sure that was it. Instead of Doug and/or Martin, though, I ended up talking to Father Grimaldi,

which was kind of a strange experience. Grimaldi asked if I had gone to see a cardiologist and that's when I realized that my first instinct was to go to a priest and not to a doc. I thought about that a lot, what that meant, then went to a cardiologist, found out it was gas.

I can't imagine Dierdre hanging onto friends for too long without having soul-searching conversations with them. In fact, if Brin and Cheryl weren't part of this crazy weight-loss thing, I wouldn't have agreed to it because I know Dierdre would talk to someone else about it and how would that look? "Hey, Jane or Carla or Sophie or Rita, guess how I got my Randy to lose weight? Promised him a roll in the hay hay hay." "And the pig agreed?" "Absolutely." "Wouldn't do it just because it was the healthy thing to do? Wouldn't do it because he loves you and wants to have a long life with you? Wouldn't do it for a million normal reasons? But he would do it so that he could dip himself into unfamiliar territory?"

Then again, I never would have met Dierdre if she didn't open herself up to, oh, anyone who would listen. I mean, I heard from five different people that she was interested in me before I actually saw her. That kind of thing happens, I don't know, let me see, never. Far as I knew I never had admirers. I was not an admiree. So when I find out this girl's attracted to me I come to the only possible conclusion: I'm thinking this girl has to have some colossal problem of one kind or another.

Which is why, when I was out with a couple of my friends at a club—this was in college—and we met up with a group of people who knew someone in our group and it was too loud to hear which someone knew someone else and who everyone was, I had no idea that this woman I was fascinated by and flirting with and dancing with and buying drinks for was the same Dierdre who had been asking everyone I know about me.

Go figure.

Out of that group of people I met at the club, out of all the people I met at every club I've ever been to, out of all the people I met since I started sprouting pubic hair, Dierdre is the one *I* wanted. And I'm the one she wanted. We were like this mutual-wanting society.

And if she—the woman I wanted and want and will be wanting until I drop dead—wants me to have sex with Brin's friend, who am I to argue?

I wouldn't want to disappoint her and stuff, she being the love of my life and all.

It's the only polite thing to do, really.

I am a pig.

DOUG 306 POUNDS

The one and only wet dream I ever remember having in my life was about a fat chick. I don't remember much except that she was wearing a breastplate like the wife in "Hagar the Horrible." I was something like sixteen at the time and had never been to the opera so it couldn't have been that.

RANDY 301 POUNDS

Okay, so I'm a pig.

But if I lose the weight, damn it, why shouldn't I get the prize?

Who is it hurting?

Especially if I don't learn the woman's name.

That's the trick. Keep it anonymous.

Dierdre and I can renew our vows before. And maybe after.

To: MBB@yahoo.com, Randy12479@aol.com
From: Doug@linklink.com,
Subject: Side bet

Side bet. First one to drop twenty-five is the only one allowed
to get a blow job from the hooker.

—Doug

Doug E. Garrison, Sales Manager
T.H.E. Solutions, "Better people through business"
One Park Plaza

***This e-mail is the property of T.H.E. Solutions and is subject
to scrutiny accordingly. This account is strictly for professional
use only.***

To: Randy12479@aol.com, Doug@linklink.com,
From: MBB@yahoo.com,
Subject: Side bet

That's really putting the honor system to the test.
  I'm in.

—Martin

To: Doug@linklink.com, MBB@yahoo.com
From: Randy12479@aol.com
Subject: Side bet

Me, too.

Two questions:

1. Is a blow job standard or is that usually an optional extra like power windows?

2. Are we going to tell the wives about this and future side bets?

Pro1: They probably expected bjs to be part of the package anyway so two of us not getting them shouldn't be a problem.

Pro2: The whole point of this craziness is to motivate us to lose weight, so why should they object to extra motivating factors?

Con1: I really don't want to talk to Dierdre about details.

Con2: The more we talk with each other about this, the less I like it, which I know isn't really a con regarding telling our wives about the bj side bet, but it is something I thought I should mention.

—Randy

"Winning's like losing, only fun."

To: MBB@yahoo.com, Randy12479@aol.com
From: Doug@linklink.com,
Subject: Side bet

Randy, you sure know how to take all the fun out of a side bet.

I vote for not telling.

—Doug

Doug E. Garrison, Sales Manager
T.H.E. Solutions, "Better people through business"
One Park Plaza

To: Randy12479@aol.com, Doug@linklink.com,
From: MBB@yahoo.com,
Subject: Sorry

Hope you guys aren't pissed, but after Doug's first e-mail I told Brin about the side bet. She got a strange look on her face, then smiled and was like "whatever works." So you'd better tell Dierdre and Cheryl—unless you want to cancel the side bet.

—Martin

To: MBB@yahoo.com, Randy12479@aol.com
From: Doug@linklink.com,
Subject: Side bet

Told Cheryl.
  In Fucking Scrutable.

RANDY 294 POUNDS

And so Dierdre said to me—and this is exactly what she said because I memorized it for future use, in fantasies and so on—"I know you'll win the side bet—but just in case, I want to make sure you get a prize."

Damn, man.

MARTIN 312 POUNDS

Walking isn't going to do it. I know that. But it's going to help. It's got to. I'm walking before work and I'm walking after dinner and I'm walking around the office complex during lunch. Trying to get as much of it in before winter hits and it's already getting colder and I don't want to be out here walking in Gore-Tex. There's only so much a man can take. Already I'm the fat guy walking around Fake Lake and I know that behind the tinted windows of the what-the-hell-do-they-do companies there are people looking out at the fat guy tsking about how they've seen it before.

Usually it's right after New Year's when all the fat folks have some sort of resolution to fit into a bathing suit by summer. So they loop around Fake Lake for a couple of weeks and then disappear in February, back to the Burger King drive-thru (just make a left out of the office complex and turn right at the light and go down a quarter mile).

I did that once, three years ago. Made a resolution. Told Brin that this was the year. Meant it, too. Was convinced that my life was a' changin'. That I was at a turning point.

Fake Lake is surrounded by companies that all sound like they could do battle against Godzilla.

Godzilla vs. Mentaldon, Godzilla vs. RahedTech, Godzilla vs. Balladin.

I pass each one of them in my fifteen-minute odyssey around Fake Lake. My boring-as-hell fifteen-minute odyssey. My focus-and-accept-that-you-will-get-to-the-end-eventually odyssey.

I've got to bring a Walkman next time. Only problem is, wearing a Walkman sends the message that I think that this is exercise. Which it is, I know, but it just looks bad if it seems like I think it is. Why do people make fun of the fat people running, the fat people at the gym, the fat people in the ball game? Isn't that what the thin world should want the fat world to be doing?

I don't think Randy's going to make it. Of the three of us, he's the one who shovels the food in when he gets nervous. The one who goes to the movies and becomes an eating machine. We went to the racetrack once and I never saw a guy take more trips to the concession stand. He just couldn't handle the pressure. He got pizza on the way to place his bet, peanuts on the way back, and guzzled a megadrink before every race. A wreck, he was. And a loser.

Until the last race, when he lucked into a semi long shot. On the way home, we stopped and he picked up the tab for a 1 A.M. breakfast.

There's no way Randy is going to make it.

Doug, on the other hand, has a shot, although he's heftier than either of us at the moment. I think. I hope. At least, he seems bigger. Might be his chest. He's fat in the chest. But he seems to have the drive to succeed at this. Yesterday he said to me, "Would you do the same for Brin? I mean, if she was so fat she could kick at any minute, would you be willing to set her up with some stud if you thought it might save her life?"

I didn't answer him.

CHERYL

Hey. First of all, I'm not going to continue being your walking buddy if you keep walking so fast. You're a freaking machine, Brin. It's like you're set at a slightly different speed than everyone else. We're all floating through life like it's a John Woo action sequence and meanwhile you're zipping past like a Benny Hill girl. I seriously don't know how you do it. I bet you're the only married couple in the world where the guy doesn't have to work not to come before you do.

Seriously? No, I was just guessing. Damn. I should find a way to make money off my intuition.

My second thing is that I'm not going to continue to be your walking buddy if we have to keep calling it "walking buddies." But that's a minor issue, a consequence of my low whimsy tolerance, no biggie.

Yeah, see, that's still too fast.

Okay, better.

So this thing, where they're now having side bets? I just want to say: hello? Since when is this supposed to be fun for them? They're taking our evil plan—sorry, your evil plan—this Machiavellian plot predicated on their being doomed to failure, and they're making it all about male camaraderie and shit like that? Not cool, B. Especially since, if they start enjoying it on any level, Christ, they could conceivably lose the weight. All the weight. And then the bedrock of our entire scheme, our faith in their being complete failures, crumbles. And then I don't know what happens except I'm pretty sure it's going to involve our changing our names and leaving town in the middle of the night and winding up as a topic on 20/20. "Lying Wives Who Lie and Leave," or something. John Stossel, reporting. I hate that guy.

Okay, now you're going too slow. You patronizing me, now? Knock it off or I'll pinch you.

So I had a bad conversation with Doug last night. You'd think I'd have learned my lesson by now, right? And just stopped trying to have conversations? It rarely ends well. But we're sitting there, him with the remote, me with my book, and I'm not reading because I'm thinking, and my thinking leads regrettably to my speaking, and thus I spake: "Hey, hon. Wacky question. You think we're happy?"

Yeah, he gives me that look. Same look he gives me if, say, I ask him to carry something heavy upstairs.

I continue. "I mean, I know we're not happy happy, not happy like the people on TV are happy, not like fictional-character happy. And I know we're happier than homeless people or people in prison camps. But in realistic terms, in relative, comparative terms, what do you think? Happy/not happy? Where on the continuum, you think?"

What did he say? He asked me if I was trying to drive him to eat. Trying to undermine our deal by making him so crazy he just has to ingest some kind of processed sponge cake with cream filling.

I wasn't, but not a bad idea. Something to bear in mind in case, against all odds, the fellas actually start closing in on 210 pounds.

No, you're right, unlikely. I shouldn't dwell.

Oh, he didn't answer the question. I don't know why I thought he would want to discuss the question. Have I never met my husband?

I guess I knew he wouldn't answer the question . . . come to think of it, I think maybe I didn't even want to discuss the question. I think maybe, I don't know, I was trying to gauge something else. Not how happy we are. I know we're not that happy. At least, not together. Separate, I think we're pretty happy. I'm happy right now, for instance, and most of the time when I'm hanging around with you (when you're not being overly weird or sinister, that is), and when I'm in the car silently heaping scorn on the people who call in to radio shows, and when I'm drawing, which I don't do that much anymore, and also when I'm watching *Queer Eye*.

So I'm sure Doug is perfectly happy, too, when we're not together. When he's with Martin and Randy, or when he's watching waitresses at lunch.

I think what I was feeling around for was evidence that there's still some magnetism there. Not magnetism. Adhesive. Whatever's sort of Velcroed us together for the past hundred and fifty years (okay, it's only been nine, but it feels longer). I'm pretty sure Doug would fall apart, cease to be, become a particularly annoying homeless guy if I weren't around. Guess I was fishing around for some confirmation of that. My women's studies prof from college would bludgeon me with an Andrea Dworkin book to hear me say it, but I guess thinking that Doug relies on me sort of keeps me going. Do I suck?

Didn't get it, anyway. The confirmation. What'd I get instead? "Cheryl, you're a fucking loon, you know that?"

Some couples do flowers or boxes of chocolate. We have our own way, Doug and I.

C'mon, B, speed up, this isn't a scenic tour. We're not ambling buddies. Show me the meaning of haste, you pussy.

MARTIN 314 POUNDS

I think I've got it figured out.

When I have the TV on in the kitchen in the morning, I keep refilling the cereal bowl until all of the milk is gone from the bowl. I stay even longer if Katie Couric is wearing a skirt.

At night, I'll park in front of the screen at seven thirty and sometimes stay there until ten, when I go upstairs to lie in front of the bedroom tube. On weekends, forget it. If I don't have a specific task around the house, there's always something on.

So here's what I have to do: eliminate TV from my life.

Or, at least, seriously cut back on TV.

No. Eliminate it.

If I'm going to do this, I have to do it.

Then, with that TV time, I have to do stuff.

I'm not sure what, but whatever I do has to be better for me than watching TV.

RANDY 293 POUNDS

If matter is neither created nor destroyed, where the hell is the ten pounds of tire that used to be wrapped around my gut? Okay, so there's still a tire there, but a tire that's ten pounds smaller than the previous tire.

MARTIN 314 POUNDS

All TV except for *The Daily Show*. Gotta watch *The Daily Show*.

RANDY 292 POUNDS

Some things I am curious or concerned about:

1. How long after I hit 210 (assuming I get there) is this thing supposed to happen? We didn't discuss specifics and I'm not sure if Dierdre would really want me to ask for details. So I've got to try to logic this out myself. Well, okay, for one thing, I'm sure this woman isn't on retainer. Given that, the next sensible question is:

2. How far in advance do you need to book a specific hooker when you want her for an entire evening? (Dierdre did say that the deal was that I could spend the night with her. The whole night, what? Talking? Cuddling? Watching cable? I mean, I'm not a machine, and I'm not as young as I used to be. And even when I was as young as I used to be, it was never an all-night activity.) I'm sure if it was just an hour appointment, she could squeeze me in. It's like a doctor, I figure. Sometimes there are complications and you fall behind. Other times you go through a few quicker than you expect and catch up a little. That's all speculation, of course, but still:

3. How long do I have to stay under 210? What happens if I get there, then put back on a few. We never talked about a minimum stay at 210. And . . .

4. Does Brin have a deal with this woman that she'll handle all of us in a three-day weekend? If that's the

case, what order do we go in? If I'm dropping a zillion pounds, I sure as hell don't want to go third. Then again, I don't expect us all to get to the magic number in the same week. If we do all finish, it could be spread out over months. There's no deadline, as far as I know. Might take forty years. Following only what was stated, I could be a withered old guy and fall below 210 and still have my shot. Then again, she'd be a withered old woman at the time—but so would Dierdre.

5. Never thought about it before, but do old guys who marry old women really like how old women look or do they just figure that's all they can get? Will I still be aware when we are, like in our eighties, that this prostitute woman (no doubt retired by then) is more attractive than Dierdre? I'm not saying that I'm not attracted to Dierdre. I am. But if I'm being honest, I have to say that being attracted to someone and that person being attractive are two different things. This occurred to me once when Dierdre was late coming home from work and I was concerned about her and I imagined myself calling the police. Of course, I would have to give a description, but in my fantasy, the cop asked me point-blank, "Would you describe her as very, very attractive? A major hottie?" Her life may depend on my description, so what do I say? "No, not really." Of course, I could have skipped the question—and guilt, and whatnot—by giving the cop a photo of her. I've got hundreds. But that's beside the point. You shouldn't avoid a major ethical question—or whatever this is—on a technicality. I assume. I'm no ethicologist. The real problem is, I've lost all objectivity

about Dierdre's looks. The only thing I can trust is the fact that I still have the major hots for her. Which one would think is all that should matter. At least to me. Still, if a magazine art director was looking for one person to feature in its Special Hot Hot Hot Issue, I think the prostitute would get the gig before Dierdre. But, then again, Dierdre would get the gig before Brin or Cheryl or even Amy. Way way before. That's just my opinion, of course. I haven't asked Doug or Martin. Probably just as well. The good thing, though, is that Brin and Cheryl and Dierdre are all in the same approximate attractiveness ballpark. I think Martin and Doug would agree with that if the subject ever came up. Which it won't. If I had to chose between Cheryl and Brin, though, well, that would be tough. That would be really tough. Jeez. If you were picking from pictures, probably Brin. If you hung out with both of them for the evening, though, like if you were on one of those dating shows that are on late at night and the idea was you had to hang out with the wives of two of your friends, then at the end of the show pick the one you wanted to hang out with alone, I think I'd have to go with Cheryl. There's something about her. Especially when she used to get really wiseass. She doesn't do that so much anymore. Now, more often it's like she thought of a joke or something smart and funny to say but she stops it right before it comes out and keeps it all in there. My guess is there's still a lot of stuff in her that doesn't come out. Not with Doug, anyway. Why is that attractive? Because maybe she'd let it out with me and that's a complimentary thing? Meanwhile I couldn't hang with Brin.

She's got all that intelligence that creates a big space between her and everyone else. What was I talking about again? This was supposed to be a list of . . . what? Something. Something. Something. Damn. I'm lost in this one. Something about questions about the whole hooker night thing. Something like that. Okay, what else? Well, how about:

6. What happens if I lose a limb in an accident? Okay, it's unlikely, but picture some storm happening and the cat runs out the door when I'm coming in and I have to go look for the thing and a bolt of lightning strikes the tree in the backyard and a limb comes down with such force that it knocks off my arm. Okay, maybe it couldn't do that now that I think about it, but it could crush my arm to a point where the dangling mass was worthless and it was better to just remove the whole thing just below the shoulder. My arm must weigh, what? Twenty-five, maybe thirty pounds. That would only leave a couple of missed meals to put me at goal weight. Would that weight loss count in Brin's game? Does Stumpy here still get the whore?

7. I can't help but wonder how much we are paying this woman. Does Brin get a friends' discount? And is she passing along any savings to Cheryl and Dierdre or is she just taking a reduced rate for herself? Back when Martin and Brin were first dating and we'd all go out, they used to always insist on splitting the check even though Dierdre and I would only have a beer or two while they'd polish off a bottle of decent wine. They never, ever seemed to notice that we were getting rooked, and the first time I told a waiter "separate checks," they

gave me a look that I thought was going to burn a hole in my skull. Dierdre reamed me out about it later that night but since then we've split checks and I figure I've saved something like four hundred bucks. But Brin may be taking all that back on the deal here. Or . . . she may be getting it for free. After all, it's not like the hooker's going to have to huppity hump three fat guys. It could actually be fun for her. Maybe she gets a kick out of married guys. For her, it's great sex without the risk that the guy is going to stalk her or want to take her to Starbucks for a latte afterward. (Great sex, okay, maybe I overestimate.)

8. Does Dierdre keep a diary or something? I think she started one a couple of years ago. Someone got it for her for her birthday but I only remember her writing in it for a month. Reason I wonder is, what if she writes all this down and, in fifty or sixty years, we both are found dead in our Florida retirement village and Ty, weeping about suddenly being an orphan, is handed this diary as if it's going to give him spiritual insight into the life of his parents and, in the limo on the way to the cemetery, he opens it up and lands in the section where Mom sends Dad to the whorey-whore?

9. I could use a latte right now.

10. Or a mocha.

DOUG 304 POUNDS

I got on the scale six times today.

    This isn't the way to do it. What I have to do is *not* get on the scale. Then get on it when the scale isn't expecting it. Use surprise to my advantage.

MARTIN 314 POUNDS

And ball games. If I have to miss ball games, what the hell's the point?

I need a remote that will block everything but *The Daily Show* and ball games. Not ball games. Let's say, sporting events. That way, hockey is included. And a lot of the Olympics that don't have to do with balls.

When is the next Olympics anyway?

RANDY 291 LBS

Apparently they've changed the rules at Weight Watchers. Back after Dierdre had Ty and wanted to lose, what'd she say, "a few postpartum pounds," she attended a couple of months of meetings and they had this whole "exchange" system that made dinner with her like eating with a commodities broker. You had to count up points for everything you ate and you had a certain amount of these "exchanges" that you could use in a week. It wasn't just like "one hamburger." It was like "three bread exchanges and two protein exchanges and three fruit exchanges." On my birthday she gave me a blow job and she couldn't eat peanut butter for a week.

She'd go to meetings and report on what she ate and I guess it worked because she dropped the weight pretty quickly.

But I don't want to go there because, well . . .

1. I don't like talking to strangers.

2. If the reason I'm going is because it worked for Dierdre but now the system has changed, that kind of screws up the endorsement, doesn't it?

3. As I think Cheryl said once, "portion control" sounds like a government department in a communist country.

4. If it's all about controlling how much you eat, why the hell do I have to pay them to do that? I can get the

information off the Internet. Or I can just cut back on what I eat, which is what I've been doing. Instead of three slices of pizza for lunch yesterday, I had two. And I didn't finish the crusts. I keep a couple of pieces of fruit with me now and eat them whenever I'm tempted to go to the candy machine. I'm not having a bowl of cereal before bed anymore. Instead, I'm brushing my teeth around nine thirty and ending my eating day right there. The results? I don't know. I don't want to hop on the scale every five minutes.

5. It feels like the right time to jump to a new number, so this will be number five. Tomorrow, I'm going to see if Ty wants to shoot some hoops.

MARTIN 312 POUNDS

I think there were entire months when I didn't eat a single piece of fruit.

DOUG 303 POUNDS

Keep. Going. Keep. Going. Keep. Going. Can't. Quit. Little. Longer. Feel. Like. Shit. Please. Death. Take. Me. Now.

I can't believe there are people who do this every day of their lives. By, like, choice.

Maybe if you do it for long enough it starts to feel good.

Maybe if you spend enough years doing it you forget what feeling good feels like. The pain and discomfort come and you're like, "Oh, yeah, I remember these guys." In the absence of anything resembling pleasure they opt for familiarity. "Pain! Discomfort! Come on in, guys, take a load off. How long has it been, about twenty-three hours? Can I get you anything? Pain, how about a chunk of my nervous system, you hungry? Discomfort, might I interest you in some of the sweat that's chafing under my waistband?"

Keep. Going. Little. Longer.

How long's it been? Six minutes. Okay. Don't look at the clock again. Don't look at the clock again.

I thought there'd be more fat people at a gym. What the fuck? Not everybody can be an "after" picture. I don't meet anybody's glance but I know what's happening when I walk through the place. "There goes the fat guy." Everyone looks at me and thinks, "Well, we know why that guy's here."

Even though they don't.

They have no idea.

They would never guess that I have tremendous self-esteem and a terrific fucking body image and that the only reason I'm here is because my wife's letting me sleep with a high-priced hooker after I lose weight. And even if they guessed that, they wouldn't guess that I don't need Cheryl's crazy offer—that I get more trim than any of the muscle junkies in here in the first place.

I get more than that guy.

Definitely more than the guy with the teeth, I don't care what his abs look like.

More than that guy.

And that guy.

Probably not more than those two guys, but that's only because I'm pretty sure they have sex with each other at the end of every spinning class.

Don't. Look. At. The. Clock. Don't. Look. At. The. Clock.

I don't know how people do it. What do they think about? What takes their mind off it? I tried listening to music with earphones like these other guys, that was ridiculous. I'm supposed to be distracted by music while I'm going through this shit? It's like someone going up to John McCain while he was in that fucking POW camp and handing him an iPod and going "Here, it's Sha Na Na." Doesn't help, thanks.

Then Cheryl gave me that book on tape that Brin gave to her, that biography of who was it, John Adams. Yeah right. Just made me loathe John fucking Adams. I hate that fucking guy. Hate anyone in a powdered wig. I think he wore a powdered wig. I didn't get that far in the book. The tape. To the hair chapter. Whatever the hell.

John friggin' Adams.

Must have sucked following Washington. Oh, we want Washington to be king. Washington won the revolution. Never told a fucking lie. Who do we put in next? I don't know, how about Adams. Friggin' Adams? Probably sick as hell of being compared to Washington. Washington wouldn't have done that. Washington would have known how to handle this. Boy, weren't things great when Washington was president?

None of that was in the book. As far as I know. Have to ask Brin. Yeah, I'll ask Brin. Like I've ever asked her anything in my life besides "You wanna hand me that bowl of chips?" Why does that woman bug me so much? Can't just be that game of Trivial Pursuit we played when we first met her. Great idea. Brilliant. "Let's play gals against guys." Dierdre's idea. I was just happy I wasn't stuck on her team. No danger of Mensa calling there. But instead Brin decides not just to show how fucking smart she thinks she is by nailing question after question, but then pulling an obvious slowdown to let us catch up. I hate the goddamn slowdown. We all know you know the fastest-swimming marine mammal, you know you know the fastest-swimming marine mammal so just admit it just fucking admit it and SAY THE FASTEST-SWIMMING MARINE MAMMAL JUST SAY IT OUT LOUD I DON'T NEED YOUR PITY MARTIN'S NEW PATRONIZING PLAYTHING SO JUST SAY IT!

And then: Fuck, I thought it was the dolphin. Fine. Just play the goddamn game and don't know so much. All bullshit anyway.

Reading something's probably not a bad idea, though. Don't. Look. At. The. Clock. Magazine or something. *Newsweek. U.S. News & World Report. Time.* Same shit. Putting them in order, I'd have to go *Time.* Then *Newsweek.* Haven't seen *U.S. News & World Report* since I switched dentists. Never quite understood why *U.S. News & World Report* never came up with a pithier name. *Time.* Four letters. *Newsweek.* Seven letters. *U.S. News* . . . No. Wait. *Newsweek* has eight letters.

Whatever the fuck. I should be reading something. Other people are reading. Some people read paperbacks while they're on the treadmill. Some people are assholes. Although it is damn funny when someone's on the treadmill reading a book and the book falls and they try to pick it up while still keeping their pace. I saw a guy the other day almost lose a kneecap. He's the only one I've seen tumble like that so far, but seeing it so early in my gym career makes me believe that it's got to happen again sooner rather than later. It's something to look forward to. Like crashes at an auto race. Whatever works.

I told Cheryl that nothing seemed to be working and, this morning, she gave me her picture of the girl, the woman we're all doing this for. Thought it might help. "Put it on the treadmill to look at while you're exercising. Like a mule with a carrot. A greyhound with a mechanical rabbit. A horny guy with a picture of a hot girl in front of him." Isn't she sweet, my wife? Always thinking of me. And such a way with metaphors. Similes, what-the-fuck-ever.

So I did it. Maybe it'll help. Maybe if I get an erection this shit won't be so awful. Couldn't hurt. Looked at her. Thought about what she must look like from the chest down. Pretty good. Probably. Her line of work. Have to. Probably. Don't look. At the clock. She's hot. Really hot. Why she does this. Her line of work. Why Brin got this idea. Why I'm here now. Because of her. Her and her. Body and her. Dimples and her. Pretty hair. If it weren't for her I. Wouldn't be here. Doing this. Don't look. At the clock. Fucking bitch. Lousy whore. Your fault bitch. Your fault whore. I hate. You. I hate. You I hate. You.

Aw. Jesus. Man. Whew.

Can look at the clock now. Now finally I can look, must be at least . . .

Seven minutes.

Fuck.

At least now I have a way to pass the time. C'mon bitch, let's go another round. Beats the hell out of listening to the Dave Matthews Band.

RANDY 288 POUNDS

It's amazing, the diets you can find on the Web. The water-and-celery diet. The chocolate-and-coffee diet. The tea-and-enemas diet. Pretty much any two things you can think of in the world, put them together and someone's made a diet out of them. Bread and water. Peas and carrots. Dog and pony. Rack and pinion. Martin and Lewis. Drunk and disorderly. Piss and moan.

I'm willing to try anything as long as it doesn't involve the word *enema*.

Or *broccoli*.

To: MBB@yahoo.com
From: Ohioguy04@aol.com
Subject: Your father

Philip, I'm looking forward to your visit this next month. Is there anything you are or aren't eating these days? Knowing that will help Brin and I stock the refrigerator. There's not much in there these days because I've gotten serious about losing weight. I just came to a point in my life where I realized that I needed to get healthier. I want to be around a good long time. It won't be long before you graduate from high school and head off to college. Regan will be close behind you. And I just decided that it's time I take better care of myself.

One thing I'm glad about is that you and Regan didn't pick up my bad eating and exercise habits. You two will never get like your old man. No way. Not that I'd have a problem with that. I would love you guys no matter what you look like. It's just that, well, you know. Unless you've got some kind of glandular thing, nobody should be as heavy as I got.

By the time you get here, I'm going to have to throw away all my old clothes. Maybe you and Regan can help me shop for new stuff. Do you do any of your own shopping now? When I was your age, I didn't want to have anything to do with clothes shopping and my mother used to buy all my clothes for me. That's why all those old pictures are so embarrassing. I look like a poster child for Sears abuse. Don't tell Grandma I said that.

Speaking of Grandma, are you still calling her every few weeks? Please try to do that. It means a lot to her.

I was hoping to hear from you on Brin's birthday a few weeks ago, but since it was a Saturday, I just assumed you were at a sleepover or something. I told Brin you called, so if it ever comes up—which it won't—tell her you're sorry she missed your call and you hope she had a nice birthday. You don't have to say it exactly like that, but you get the idea.

Please tell me what Regan is up to these days. She doesn't seem to like to talk on the phone and your mother only tells me the really big stuff and the really negative stuff. I heard when she got Student of the Month at her kindergarten and I heard when she bit your cousin, but those don't tell me much about her. Is she generally happy? Does she have a sense of humor yet? Does she ask you for advice or help with anything? Since I can't be with you—I wish more than anything that I could—at least I know that I had you in the house long enough to know you, to have a relationship. Regan doesn't even remember living with me, so I'm just this guy who she visits for a week here and a week there. I wish there was something I could do to change that but I know there isn't.

I'll stop talking about that now. You don't need to hear any of that. Just know that I love you and I think about you guys all the time. Please be helpful to Regan and be good to your mother and your aunt and your cousins. Maybe we can go canoeing this summer (now that I'm losing weight, what happened that summer on the Ohio River won't happen again, I promise) or camping or something. When I come out to pick you guys up, maybe we can go to Cedar Point again. They got a new roller coaster going in this season that looks like it's got your name on it.

And maybe while you're here we can get to Chicago for a ball game.

Brin and I love you very much. E-mail me whenever you want.

Love,
Dad.

DOUG 301 POUNDS

Ten minutes and I'm done. Ten minutes and I'm done. I hate this shit. I hate this shit. I hate this shit.

Only way to get through is to let the mind wander. Let it wander. Wander. Wander. Come on, you fucking mind, wander.

Okay, where to wander. Wander somewhere.

Music. Wander to music.

The fattest guy I ever saw in concert was Meat Loaf. The sweatiest guy I ever saw in concert, too.

What pissed me off, though, and kept me from really getting into the music was that I kept noticing my date looking at Meat Loaf, then looking at me, then looking at Meat Loaf, then looking at me. Like she was working at a fucking "guess your weight" booth and, because she knew Meat Loaf's weight from, I don't know, *People* magazine or some shit and she was using that as a standard to try to guess mine.

You know what I wanted to say to her? "The 'Paradise by the Dashboard Light' chick is creaming all over him," I wanted to say to her. "You don't look half as good as the 'Paradise by the Dashboard Light' chick (who wasn't the same one on the record). It's me who's slumming here. Not you, sweetie. You've got a fairly nice ass, but your face screws up your overall average."

Wonder what Meat Loaf is up to these days. If he

invested right, he's probably still getting laid by groupies. Groupies don't care how fat you are. You could be the chick from *What's Eating Gilbert Grape*—wait, I don't know if it applies to chicks or not. There aren't that many famous fat chicks anyway. Once they get fat I guess they stop being famous. Maybe that answers my question. Unless they're actresses gaining weight for a role, in which case it's, like, courageous. Eating Danishes and deep-dish pizza is their equivalent of rushing into burning buildings.

Anyway. Instead, let's say, the Ruben guy from *American Idol*. He got as much tail as he wanted once that album hit. Women don't have much pride when it comes to rich and famous guys. Money makes them horny. Fame makes them hornier.

Or maybe it's not horny. Maybe what I mean is, willing. 'Cause no matter what people say about women being as wild as men, I still have yet to see a chick get as horny as a guy. And the horny ones aren't as horny or as consistently horny. But if they see something they want, they know how to get it.

So Meat Loaf got laid and Ruben got laid and fucking opera singers probably get soprano blow jobs whenever they want them and the fat guy from The Fifth Dimension gets laid and so did Elvis in the later days and . . .

Great. Now I still have six minutes to go and I'm fucking horny. I've learned it's not good to have a chub while exercising. Throws off the balance.

Problem is, "Paradise by the Dashboard Light" reminds me of this other chick from high school. Never went out with her. Just gave her a ride home from a party senior year—I think she was a sophomore—and I said to her "Do you mind if we go the long way because I'm still a little buzzed and I shouldn't go home yet." She said, "If you're buzzed, maybe you should just park for a little." So we parked and we kissed and my hand went up her shirt and that's as far as it got so it was nothing at all like "Paradise by the Dashboard Light" because in that song, he's begging her for sex and she wants him to be in love with her and in this case, she didn't demand anything and I wasn't going for anything. We were parked for maybe an hour and we didn't talk about it in school the next day but it was the most satisfying relationship I've ever had. I mean that. I'm not proud of it but it's the truth.

I should Google her one of these days. I just have to dig out my yearbook to find her last name.

Three minutes. Home stretch.

What would Cheryl do if we were coming home from some forgettable restaurant or some lame movie or another night hanging with Martin and Brin and Dierdre and Randy, and I said, "Let's just park somewhere."

She'd laugh and snort and go, "Yeah, right!" She'd go, "Whatever you say, Fonzie!" Make some reference to Inspiration Point or Potsie or Pinky Tuscadero. That's what she'd fucking do.

RANDY 285 POUNDS

"Dog and pony," that could be, like, a Vietnamese diet. "The Saigon dog and pony diet."

Hee hee. Is that offensive, or just funny?

I'm going to write it down for the fellas.

MARTIN 308 POUNDS

What I want Brin to do is give me a report on how Doug and Randy are doing. She assumes that we are like her and her friends—that we talk all the time and compare notes. I don't think she really realizes that I actually work at work.

Even if I did call Doug or Randy every day, we probably wouldn't tell each other how much we lost and how hard it is and how we feel about it. This is—and I don't think our wives fully grasp this—a competition. It's as much a battle between each other as it is between us and our Heffulumpian shapes.

Or are Woozles the fat ones? Whatever. I hate trying to make clever cultural references. My boss, Henry, makes those sort of comments all the time. We'll be talking about a deal or last night's game or a restaurant that someone went to and suddenly he'll pull some Dennis Miller shit and figure out a way to work in Rerun from *What's Happening?* Or the Sylvester Stallone arm-wrestling movie or the guy who wrote *Wealth of Nations*. I can't do that because, even if something comes to mind, I get a last-minute attack of doubt that I'm remembering things wrong. That I'm going to make the wrong reference. That instead of someone from *Saved by the Bell*, the person I'm thinking of was actually on *Hanging With Mr. Cooper* or *Head of the Class*. That I'm going to say Boutros Boutros-

Ghali when I should be saying Slobodan Milosević. Or vice versa.

When did clever become more important than smart?

I'm smart. I am. Really. 1420 on my SATs.

When was the last time someone asked me what I got on my SATs?

Back when I was 190 pounds, I think. Probably Amy. Amy would have wanted to know. Amy was brilliant. Not great at pop culture references, either, but the woman knew stuff and knew how to put things together.

I don't know what Brin got on the SATs. Seems kind of late to ask her these days. If she got less than me, that kind of feels like I'm bringing it up to brag or something. If she got more than me, then . . . damn, that would probably mean she's been deliberately keeping it from me because she thought I wasn't as smart as her. And that would mean that not only does she think she's got a husband who's so fat she has to hook him up with a hooker, but also who's so dumb that she can't tell him that she got kick-ass SAT scores.

My guess is that, of the three of them, Cheryl did the best on the SATs. With some people, you just know.

Doug, on the other hand, probably blew off the test and went skiing. Then faked an injury and hung out in the lodge eating pizza. And got laid by a girl three years older than him.

DOUG 300 POUNDS

Don't look. Don't look. Don't look. I gotta look. Six minutes. I've only been at this for six minutes. Fuck. Got to get my mind occupied. Got to stop thinking about the time. Gotta take a mental vacation.

Think about: that e-mail from Randy. "Dog and pony," what's he talking about? Was that supposed to be a joke? All the weight Randy's losing is coming off his cerebellum.

Okay, that was a nonstarter. What else?

Funny guys. Fat funny guys.

There used to be lots of fat, funny guys. Curly from the Three Stooges. Louie Anderson. Lou Costello. Junior Samples from *Hee-Haw*.

There were a lot of them, I just can't think of them all right now. Buddy Hackett was kind of heavy.

Five minutes left. Just keep the legs moving for five minutes.

Now, though, what happens is, someone is heavy and funny, then he gets a sitcom and people start taking his picture and he ends up in *People* magazine and on *Entertainment Tonight* and he's got enough money for a personal trainer and a personal chef and young hotties are coming on to him and he figures he'll get even more and have more stamina and look better in the magazines if he drops a few and so he does because he can. He can hire someone to ride his ass until he drops it. Someone to

the high-impact infidelity diet

slap his hand when he goes for the Snickers bar. And so he drops the pounds and he's not as funny as he was before, but he doesn't have to be because he's made a shitload of money and he's getting laid on a regular basis.

That's what I need. A sitcom.

And to figure out a way to get rid of the image of Lou Costello having sex.

To: BrinM@compumail.net
From: Chercher@worknet.com
Subject: RE: You suck

Okay, first of all I shouldn't even be talking to you (and by "talking," of course, I mean "typing," and by "typing" I mean "hunting and pecking while feverishly suppressing bad memories of high-school keyboarding class"). You said you'd come to the neighborhood association meeting last night. You said you'd be my buffer, my coconspirator, an audience for my worst impulses.

Instead, you wisely stayed home. While I had to go. I told you why I had to go. I had to go because Jill next door cornered me last weekend when I was getting the mail and asked if I was going to go, said she really thought I ought to go, and because last year she gave us cookies, cookies Doug and I couldn't bring ourselves to eat (*Doug* couldn't eat! Cookies Doug *could not eat!*) but also never reciprocated; I had no leverage and was in her debt and must do her bidding. She's like Suburbio Corleone, this woman.

So, my friend Brin, hereinafter referred to as lying slut, here's what you missed:

For one thing, Jill was wearing socks that had snowmen on them. Kept crossing her legs so we could all appreciate them. I argue that it would be better to live in a state that punished people for wearing such socks, even if a few other civil liberties got swept up in the process. Sign my petition later.

Owen Libby on Brokenhurst is still having a conniption about the color of the Campbells' new garage. Keeps saying "It's not a color found in nature!" News flash, Mr. L: your too-short pants are made of a fabric not found in nature. And I'm not sure nature would smile on whatever that is you're doing with your comb-over either. It's definitely a crime against physics.

Kept wondering why I'd been urged to come. Assumed it was Jill's attempt to force me to simulate a neighborly civility we fail to demonstrate every time we don't participate in the July-Fourth-decorations contest. Then the meeting moves on to the next order of business: the Winter Festival. (You know, what they used to call the Christmas Festival until the Bernsteins moved in on Graham Road?) There's going to be a parade down the middle of the "hopefully snowy" street (they're praying for snow, these people; it's like they're pagan slush worshipers). And the festivities will climax with the arrival of Santa Claus, in a sleigh, drawn by God knows what—terriers? teamsters?—a big fat man in a red suit handing out cheap but festive presents to all the neighborhood children assembled.

Everyone nodded, basking in what a great idea it was, and then everyone slowly sort of turned and looked at me. Took me a second to figure out why. Then I remembered: Oh, right, I have the fattest husband!

(Another reason why I NEEDED YOU TO BE THERE!)

Got out of it. Said Doug couldn't possibly play Santa because he's a misanthropist. No one understood. Then I said we don't do Christmas and that we're Muslim. Everyone got uncomfortable and moved on to the next order of business.

So, questions for you: 1. Want our Christmas tree? 2. When is Ramadan? 3. What is Ramadan?

Loveyameanit,

C.

RANDY 283 POUNDS

For the first New Year's since I don't know when, I don't need to resolve to lose weight. I'm already doing it. I don't know what to do with my New Year's resolution responsibilities. If everyone in America lost weight, I think the New Year's resolution tradition would go the way of, what, Arbor Day parties.

So what? Watch less TV? That's dumb. That would kind of mean that watching TV is a bad thing, and how can anything that gives so much pleasure be that bad?

Something about work? Work harder at work? Be more ambitious? Doug said once it seemed like I'd been assistant coach forever. But danged if I'm going to make resolutions to please Doug.

Maybe it should be something that will help me when I've lost all the weight and get the prize. Learn some new moves for Brin's friend. I hear people talk about moves and I don't know what they mean. I don't even have one move, just sort of a, I don't know, a shudder. Growing up, nobody ever said anything about needing to know moves, nowadays I'm supposed to be, what, Baryshnikov in there?

I resolve to learn some moves.

Done. Moving on.

MARTIN 295 POUNDS

Must have been two in the morning. She fell asleep with the TV on and I figured she was out cold so I shut it off without doing what I usually do, which is turn the volume down first, make sure she's out, and then click it off. This time, I went right to the click and it proved to be a major mistake.

"What's wrong?" she asked groggily.

"Nothing. Go back to sleep."

"What?"

"It's okay."

"Are you okay?"

"Yes. Everyone's okay. Got to sleep."

"I'm up now."

And she was. That's all it takes. Then the TV goes back on and it's an *E! True Hollywood Story* already a third of the way done, which means that we skip over the awkward childhood and the shots of whoeverthehell in her high school play. I don't even recognize the actress this time. Someone from a '90s sitcom, I think, which is a time when my sitcom knowledge pretty much drops out. I'm pretty good with '70s and '80s. Quiz me on *All in the*

Family and *Welcome Back Kotter* and I'm gold—provided it's a straight-up quiz and not an off-the-cuff pop culture reference. But the '90s are a blur. Maybe I got more selective in my TV watching. Maybe my memory is deteriorating. Did we really think she was hot back then, whoever that is? Is that what passed for masturbation material ten years ago?

I want to make a little bit of a move on Brin, but I don't want her to think that this actress is doing it for me. I don't want her to think that while making love with her, I'm thinking about Judith Light—maybe that's who it is, Judith Light. Didn't she do that show with Tony Danza? This has to be the worst *E! True Hollywood Story* of all time.

We've made love three times since the deal and every time I imagine that Brin's thinking that I'm thinking about the hooker woman. I'm not, though. I barely got a look at the photo—just enough of a peek to know she's hot but not enough to retain an image. Besides, that picture was taken ten years ago. I'm not saying that a thirty-year-old woman can't be hot. Of course she can. My wife is hot. In a thirty-four-year-old wifey kind of way. But what I'm saying is that there's not enough material there for me to fantasize about, particularly when I'm making love with my wife, who I'm attracted to most of the time, particularly when we're going at it.

I let my foot touch hers.

"Cold," she says, but doesn't pull away.

For a week, about a year ago, she tried sleeping naked. Somebody told her that it was better for her in some way and she would wear her pajamas until she climbed in. For her, the problem—the thing that kept her from staying with the plan—was the cold. At least, she thought it was the cold. It couldn't have been, though. There's no way in hell the flimsy material of her pjs could actually keep her warm.

But she felt more comfortable in them than she did out of them so she put them back on.

To me, the problem was different. The problem was that things change when suddenly, every night, there's a naked woman lying next to you. It's like the signal at an intersection is broken and the drivers (in this analogy, that's my penis and me), don't know when to proceed. In the past, both with Brin and with Amy before her, the point of nudity was the point when the green light was bright. During Brin's naked period, though, we were about as happy as two people swapping insurance information by the side of the road.

Truth is, though, the nude-at-night thing didn't really work for me anyway. I didn't realize it until then, but I have an aesthetic preference for the still-attached article of clothing. The loose T-shirt. The socks. The hiked skirt. The necklace. I got a version of that kick in the mornings, when I woke up, by carefully moving blankets while she slept, created some pretty pleasing semi-still lifes.

But then I made assumptions. Usually wrong assumptions. Now she wears her pjs. And when they come off, things are a' happenin'.

One more lesson in the art of marriage. Even after Amy, I had no friggin' clue there was this much still to learn.

In my first marriage, I learned that a honeymoon was a honeymoon. I knew that kids would slow things down, as would work and other bullshit. And I knew that my growing girth would eventually seriously diminish Amy's "oh, baby, give it to me" desires of once upon a time.

But I didn't know that I'd be negotiating and strategizing with Brin as much as I have over the past couple of years. We've been married for five years now, and I thought, really thought, that by this time I would know what she wanted and when she wanted it. This batlike sonar, this spider sense, this ESP, would lead to giggly rendezvous in coat closets and seriously intense run-ins at the office. Barring that, I thought I would at least know how to ease her toward those carnal points and maximize my chances of a satisfying missionary encounter on a given evening.

So, Judith Light, or whoever the hell it is, and her rising career be damned, I go for it.

I let my foot go farther up her leg.

I kiss her on the neck.

I feel her hand reach around me and I try to forget how substantial I am. Try to forget the time I was on top of her and she screamed out in pain because I put my weight down on her thigh. Try to forget that when she sucks me she might as well be hiding out behind a bunker.

I let it all go and rather than imagining her as anybody else, I imagine myself as, well, not someone else— as me in nine months. Or a year.

"Hmmmm," she says as she pulls me toward her, "you lost weight."

My body smiles.

DOUG 297 POUNDS

I knew the Super Bowl would suck this year. I didn't know how badly.

It started in the first quarter when the apple slices were already turning brown and the peanut butter was sitting on the untouched celery and the room was just screaming for Fritos and barbecued potato chips and a big sloppy plate of nachos buried in cheese and jalapeños and beans that would make the third act an Olympian fart fest.

Martin didn't want to be the first to complain. Randy didn't want to be the first. Somebody had to.

"This fucking sucks," I said.

"Not a bad game," said Randy and, as usual, I didn't know if he was trying to be funny or he was really that clueless. "Good commercials."

Ever since everyone in the world started paying attention to the commercials—ever since the halftime show became such an over-the-top bullshit extravaganza—the game hasn't been the same. Still, that wasn't what I was talking about.

"Not the game, dickhead. I'm talking about the apples and the celery and the salad, for Christ's sake. Who the hell has a salad while watching the Super Bowl?"

"I made the salad," said Randy, a little defensively.

"You don't make a salad," I said and probably shouldn't

have. "You throw lettuce and shit in a bowl. That's not *making*."

"Do you *make* nachos?" asked Martin, trying to start an argument.

"Doesn't matter," I said. "They're nachos. You don't have to think about nachos. You don't have to put words to it. You don't even have to be good at it. You just have to eat it DURING THE FIRST QUARTER OF THE GOD-DAMN SUPER BOWL."

"All right," said Randy, deliberately keeping his eyes on the screen even though it was a time-out.

"By the second quarter," I continued, "they've got to get kind of nasty but there's still like one or two whole chips left that are buried in cheese but you pick it up anyway. By halftime it's just gross but you get kind of desperate and you go in anyway because you have to. You have to. In the fourth quarter, you can't even look at them."

"And you miss that?" asked Randy.

"Abso-fucking-lutely."

"Damn straight," added Martin. "But the trick is to convince yourself that none of that stuff exists. Those Wendy's ads on TV are just more fictional programming. Those White Castle bags are filled with balls of pure fat. Bite into one of those burgers and it's like biting into the flab under your grandmother's arm."

"That's disgusting," I said.

"Right. That's the point," said Martin, and I was start-ing to get what he was saying. "It's not only illegal to have nachos while watching the Super Bowl. It's also a proven fact that every plate of nachos is covered with phlegm. Phlegm hocked up from the throat of the fat girl from *The Facts of Life*. That's what you gotta do to get by."

I never thought of Martin as a wordsmith, but I was tempted to write that shit down. He had something there.

"Enough," said Randy.

"No," I said. "Keep going."

"Nothing else to say," said Martin.

"Give me one more disgusting one?" I said.

"Okay," said Martin. "Pick a food."

"Please stop," said Randy. "I'm asking you to stop."

"Ribs," I said.

"Okay, ribs," said Martin. "You don't want to eat ribs because they are the ribs of your dead parents."

"No!"

"I'm going to throw up," said Randy.

"That's what they do on sausage pizzas," said Martin. "They make the little chunks of sausage out of little chunks of vomit. There's a special coagulator they use to keep them together."

"I'm leaving," said Randy, but he didn't get up.

We watched the game for a few minutes.

"Any of you guys try throwing up?" Martin asked.

"Like Karen Carpenter you mean?" That was me asking. But I wasn't sure if she was one of those people who threw up or one of those people who didn't eat. I never could remember which was anorexic and which was bulimic. It's like stalactites and stalagmites with me. Never could keep them fucking straight.

"Not me," said Randy. "How about you?"

"Thought about it," said Martin. "Haven't tried it. Haven't really thrown up since Randy's bachelor party."

"I did once," I told them. "Early in the thing when I didn't feel like the exercise was getting anywhere. I had just eaten a sandwich—not even a really fattening one—but I figured if I already had the pleasure of eating it, why not get rid of it and ditch some of the calories? Went into the restaurant bathroom and tried to hold my tongue down and just gagged until I heard the door open and someone come in."

I was going to tell them more, but then there was a fumble on a punt return and by the time things in the game calmed down it seemed stupid to continue. There's a time for these things. A window. A second where you either say something or you don't, you either do something or you don't, you either stick your finger down your throat or you don't, you either tell your friends about it or not, you either put up a fight to keep your kids or, like Martin, you don't. You either eat that extra slice of pizza or you don't.

RANDY 283 POUNDS

I can't even look at nachos on TV anymore. I know I can't eat them anyway, but still, it's not right. It's like taking away a man's god or something, and you don't do that.

DOUG 293 POUNDS

Here's what pisses me off: Martin is looking good.

Not that I think he's hot or anything. I'm not that way, and he wouldn't be my type anyway. It's just that I saw him the other day and I did a double take.

Here's what would be humiliating: He wins this thing and I don't.

Or he wins this thing and I finish, like, six months later. I'm giving it to a hooker who's six months older than the hooker who fucked Martin. That would suck.

Randy I'm not worried about. Randy's going to drop twenty-five and Dierdre's going to act like he suddenly became Adonis. She's already all over him like white on rice and a few pounds will only make it worse. All his worshipful shit will kick into even higher gear and he wouldn't think of banging another chick, even if wifey approves.

Besides, Dierdre is kind of hot. They're like one of those fat guy/hot chick sitcoms. You can't imagine the King of Queens dude fucking around on the whatever-her-name-is Queen of Queens. On the other hand, you can easily imagine her—the Queen of Queens chick—mixing it up with some cable guy.

Which makes you wonder if Dierdre and her breasts of wonder ever did a little on-the-side rockin' and boppin'. Or if she did, would she stop once fatty Randy got down to size?

Which he won't.

Not a chance.

Even if he does miraculously manage to get down to 210. He'll say "no thank you" and then Martin and I will have to say "no thank you" and the wives will have won.

No, they won't. Fuck 'em. Even if Randy takes a pass on the reward, I'm going to go for it. Martin can decide for himself—but he'll probably cower, too, because he'll be so afraid that Brin will walk the way Amy walked.

So not only will I spend the night with hookergirl, I'll also be the only one of us who does.

Game.

Set.

Match.

To: BrinM@compumail.net
From: Chercher@worknet.com
Subject: RE: RE: The Plan

LOSE WEIGHT NOW, ASK US HOW!

Atkins is a loser. South Beach is washed up. Tae-Bo is for pussies. Bo-Tae is a pasta. Sign up now for the ONLY PROVEN METHOD to LOSE WEIGHT FAST and FEEL BETTER ABOUT YOURSELF and GET YOUR WIFE OFF YOUR BACK.

It's the weight-loss sensation that's sweeping the nation: the Brin-Cher Low-Fat Harlot Diet. Through a CAREFULLY CALIBRATED DIET of carbs, protein, nutritional supplements, and one skanky ho, you can go from fat to phat in a matter of weeks! Just have a diet shake for breakfast, another shake for lunch, and then a sensible slattern for dinner. THE POUNDS WILL MELT AWAY!! True, they'll be replaced by shame and self-loathing, but those don't weigh anything and they won't keep you from fitting in your old letter jacket.

Brin-ster,
Just wanted to point out that after all is said and done we could have a lucrative career ahead of us as spammers. We've already got weight loss and sex factored into our scheme; figure out a way to work in debt consolidation, penis enlargement, and an attractive financial offer from Dr. Phil Nguyobe of the Ivory Coast and we've got a surefire winner.

Doug's losing weight. He looks terrific. And he no longer heads off to the gym with the look of a stray dog on its last day at the pound. Tell me again; when are they supposed to

hit these plateaus you were promising? Just wondering because if I need to transition from smug elation to panic I
should pencil it in on my calendar.

Yrs in giddy despair,

C.

—·—

Randy,

This Post-it is to remind you of how proud I am that you're getting so back into shape!!! I love it!!! Mowr!!

                                        Dierdre

Randy,

This Post-it is to explain, I don't think I spelled that right, it was supposed to be a sound like a cat makes, not a little meow but you know like a sexy sound like people make.

This Post-it is to continue where the last Post-it cut off, they're small!!!

Like a sexy sound like people make in the movies. Rowr, or Mowrowr, anyway, it's supposed to be a sexy sound. Purrrr.

Randy,

This Post-it is in your shoe to remind you of how much I love you with all my SOLE!! HA!!!!

Dierdre

Randy,

This Post-it is in your lunch bag to re-mind you of the reason why you're eating these baby carrots instead of eating that other stuff with the team.

Those are supposed to be breasts. Brin's friend's ample, heaving, supple, warm breasts. Keep your mouth off those fried fish sandwiches and you can put your mouth on these, her nipple stiffening hotly under the urgent pressure of your teeth and if you want I can watch.

Dierdre

Randy,

This Post-it is in your wallet because you're MONEY to me, baby! HA!!

D.

Randy,

This Post-it is to say that I really hope you find these Post-its in your wallet before you find the one in your lunch bag because, if not, these are going to seem really, really anticlimactic.

D.

To: Chercher@worknet.com
From: BrinM@compumail.net
Subject: RE: Paging Dr. Freud

C,

So this morning as we're getting ready for work, Martin insists on telling me about a "horrifying" dream he had last night. The adjective he used: "horrifying." Which is how I thought I knew it was going to be either really boring, or about my family, or a little from column A, a little from column B.

In his dream he'd lost way more weight. "I was looking really good," he said. And he was getting dressed to go out. "I looked really good in my clothes. I don't know where you were," he said. And he opened the closet, apparently, to get his jacket, and there on the floor of the closet, glistening and gently jiggling, was all the fat he'd lost. Like he'd been secretly stashing it there for months. But now he'd opened the closet door and the stuff started oozing out. He tried to shove it back in with his feet, which, he said, was horrible because "I was wearing my good shoes." But it all came pouring out of the closet, viscous and irrepressible, but he had someplace to go, so he covered it up with towels and fled. In his gooey shoes. Probably tracking stuff everywhere.

When I finished laughing and wiping the tears of glee from my eyes, Martin stared coldly at me and said, "You're supposed to be horrified."

Oh, yeah, and then I think Martin got to where he was going and apparently my father was there, dressed like Don Corleone and carrying a big box of Tinkertoys.

Moral: Check the guys' closets.

—B.

RANDY 282 POUNDS

Dierdre found the list.

I was in the middle of making it when someone from her class called for her and didn't know whether or not she had his cell phone number so I wrote it on the back of the paper that I was writing the list on and forgot about it and gave it to her and, in bed, she asked me what it was. That's because I usually don't put the title at the top of a list. I just make the list, title be damned. I usually number it but not always. This practice goes all the way back to fourth grade, when I was making a list of kids I would strangle if I was the kind of kid who strangles other kids. That list was snatched by Thurman Cryer, who was somewhere around fifth or sixth on the list. When he asked me, at recess, what the deal was with the list, I acted surprised and then admitted to him it was people I was going to be inviting to a party that my mom said I could have. But then, a week later, I told him that I had gotten in trouble and the party was canceled. He wanted to know what I did to get punished, so I told him that I peed in the sink while my sister was wasting time in the bathroom and that cracked Thurman up. He thought it was the funniest thing he'd ever heard and, that day, he picked me second for his kickball team, shocking the three-quarters of the class that usually gets picked before me.

For about two and a half weeks, I was in with the in crowd.

The list that Dierdre found was as follows:

1. *Chocolate-covered pretzels*
2. *Cool Ranch Doritos*
3. *Cheap taco lunches*
4. *Dr Pepper*
5. *Nachos*
6. *Popeye's chicken*
7. *French fries (any restaurant or fast food other than Sonic)*
8. *Heavily buttered dinner rolls*
9. *Meat-lovers pizza*
10. *Stuffed-crust pizza*
11. *Pizza (other)*
12. *Marie Callender's frozen meal*

There were dozens more I could have added to the list—which, if I had given it a title, would have been called "Reasons I am going to fail." But I didn't finish it.

Dierdre understood the gist, though. She handed it back to me, saying, "I'm not sure if you needed this or not." I just muttered a thank you and waited for the other shoe, which dropped about eighteen minutes later.

"I think maybe I should start doing the grocery shopping," she said.

I didn't argue.

MARTIN 292 POUNDS

Little did I know that there was a subculture down here—a cult built around the goddamn *Price Is Right*, a show I hate with Doug-like venom.

They showed me the gym on the office tour three years ago when I got my second interview here and I remember very clearly that this same guy was here and he was watching *The Price Is Right*. I haven't been down in the basement since last week and, sure enough, there's the same guy— who I think works in Personnel—watching *The Price Is Right*. Wiry dude. Must be somewhere in the 150 to 160 range. He's here when I take my lunch break—around 12:15—and he's here when I finish up in the showers— around 12:50. Always on the Stair Climber. Always watching *The Price Is Right*. Always pissing me off.

Because I can't stay on the bike without something to focus on. I'm not wired to meditate. I'm wired to fill the time with whatever my senses can get a hold of. I swear, if I were alone, I'd masturbate on the exercise bike. At least I'd be doing something.

I've tried a magazine. I've tried a book. But nothing works like watching TV, preferably a sitcom rerun that I've already seen. *Gilligan's Island. Hogan's Heroes. Bewitched.* Don't care. Could even be *Seinfeld* or *Friends*. Doesn't matter. Gotta be an episode I've seen. Half hour goes by like nothing. Second episode airs and I'm on for an hour. I've heard once that there are some treadmills they make where you are hooked up to a video game and you can only keep playing as long as you are keeping up your pace. A little Tetris might work for me.

But not this. Mother of God, not this.

The Price Is Right is a death sentence. An eternity. Rather than get into the exercising zone, I can feel my blood pressure rise to a point where I want to take the whole freakin' PLINKO display and cram it down Bob Barker's smug "spay and neuter your pets" throat. I don't give a shit what's in the showcase. I don't give a shit if the guy in uniform beats the fat woman (she's got to be one of those 299-plus women who traditional scales can't measure). I don't give a shit who can "come on down." What I care about is grabbing the remote from the Personnel guy.

What would he do?

Really, what would he do?

I don't see a list of gym TV rules on the wall. I'm sure there's nothing in the employee manual (although, if he is from Personnel, there's a chance that he wrote it, so maybe there is). There's nobody here supervising. (There was, I'm told, when the boss first opened it. They had a fitness expert on staff. But that position dried up at the first hint of a recession.)

If I were to take the remote from him, I would have to strike strategically. First step: Casually walk over to the paper towel machine. Step two: Get a paper towel and the spray bottle of disinfectant. Step three: Casually clean off the hand grips on the bike I was using. Step four: Spray the disinfectant directly into the asshole's eyes. Step five: Grab the remote. Step six: Click.

Last week, I thought about trying the democratic route. Get a consensus. Power in numbers.

A guy from Accounting who had been working with free weights was in the locker room when I got out of the shower and I said to him, "That dude really likes *The Price Is Right*." And Accounting Dude said, "Oh, I wasn't paying attention."

Yeah, right. He wasn't paying attention? Like you could ignore it? Like this guy was so into his goddamn curls that he didn't even notice one TV in the place was blasting *The Price Is Right*?

For a minute I was more pissed at Accounting Guy then I was at Personnel Guy. It was like the women at Regan's baby group, who used to say to Amy, "Oh, we don't watch TV" or "We don't buy anything made from molded plastic." My ass you don't watch TV. My big fat double-wide ass you don't watch TV. Show me your brat in five years and tell me she's not begging for My Little Pony or whatever the hell kids will be begging for by then. Pretentious, ignorant bullshit lie.

Amy quit that group because of their bullshit. That's one of the things I loved about her. Low tolerance for bullshit. Fools not gladly suffered. Practical approach to the world. Want to say that TV is evil? Or that America sucks? Or that America can do no wrong? Or that your vegan life is the only morally correct one? Or that dogs are without question better than cats? Or that your homeopathic magnet-wielding pseudodoctor can take care of my father's cancer?

Try to pull any of that crap with Amy in the room and you are in deep. Amy will give you a look that will crush your lazy opinion faster than visions of Bea Arthur can wither an erect penis.

Brin is kind of the same way. If Brin were in my life when my father died, I'm pretty sure she would have been as strong as Amy was. Would have carried me—literally, carried me—through the service at the church. I know she would have. She would have been great.

And it's not fair for me to blame Brin for what happened with Amy. I didn't even know Brin when Amy split.

So why do I feel that she's somehow responsible? Like she had something to do with Amy leaving?

What I say to myself again and again and again is that I'm lucky. I'm the luckiest dude in the world. The woman I loved, the woman I had kids with, dumped me. Left me. Clichéd herself away with her lover and took the kids with her. And rather than turn into some Internet-porn-addicted fat-guy bachelor who never so much as kissed a woman for the rest of his life, I turned into a fat married guy with only a minor addiction to Internet porn who got to spend the rest of his life with a terrific lady who also happens to be fairly hot. How freakin' lucky is that? Forget lucky. That's miraculous.

I've got no business thinking about Amy. I've got no business being able to call up two or three dozen distinct memories of circumstances under which we made love (always starting with the seven-time day in the hotel in Amish country). No business wondering what she'll think of my revamped body. No business doing a Google photo search on her just to see if for some reason she made a local newspaper or something. No business trying to stretch out the pickup and drop-off times for the kids. No business telling Brin it was her dad who was dressed like the Godfather in my dream when really it was Amy's.

On paper, I think I've been a pretty good husband for Brin. Once I'm down to my fighting weight, there won't be too much that the outside world could take me to task for. Nice to her when we're out with other people. Still open the car door for her (when I can make it around quick enough). Don't pressure her to have sex more than she wants to (and she usually wants to about as much as I do). Listen to her stories from the office with as much interest as she listens to mine.

Brin is great. 'Til death do us part.

Yeah, that sounds right.

But sometimes, not as much as it used to be, but, still, sometimes, Amy enters my mind just before the big moment and it's not just a flash of fantasy but a fantasy-with-a-dilemma because Dream Amy realizes what she did and Dream Amy sees the error of her ways and Dream Amy will do anything—anything—to make things work again and don't I want my wife and kids and me all in the same house? Don't I want that family again? "A couple isn't a family," Dream Amy says. "What's worse," she asks, "hurting Brin or hurting your real family?" "We can make it work this time," she says. "You know I love you," she says.

And she looks gorgeous. Not like on our honeymoon gorgeous but gorgeous now gorgeous. Getting-older-with-style gorgeous. Confident and right and powerful gorgeous. And she wants me back.

And *The Price Is Right* is still on.

Dear Mr. De Niro,

I was going to start this letter by saying that I guess you get a lot of fan mail, but then I thought about it and realized you might be the kind of guy who doesn't get much fan mail at all because you have this intimidating screen presence that makes you different from guys like Hugh Grant.

Regardless, this is not a fan letter—although I am a fan. Top five De Niro performances: 1. Raging Bull. 2. Godfather Part II. 3. The Deer Hunter. 4. Goodfellas. 5. Stanley and Iris.

I know some people haven't even heard of Stanley and Iris. *But it was in frequent rotation on HBO the week I broke my leg and I watched it, in whole or in parts, five or six times. I really believed that you couldn't read and that you liked Jane Fonda and I guess that's what acting is all about.*

Before this starts to sound like a fan letter, though, I should tell you the real reason why I am writing to you.

I'm trying to lose lots of weight. I have to. And the only person I know and respect who successfully kept it off was you, after you made Raging Bull. *I mean, you beefed up to, what, 260 to play Jake La Motta? And not bulk-up stuff. You really porked out like one of us fat guys.*

Then you lost it and that's what I need to do. I don't know you so I won't tell you details but suffice it to say there's a really, really good reason why I have to get down to 210.

I look forward to hearing from you and seeing your next movie—although I think maybe you should stop for a while with the comedies. Analyze This *and* Meet the Parents *were okay, but think about what you could have done with your time rather than making* Rocky and Bullwinkle *or* Analyze That. *At least you haven't done as much crap as Pacino has.*

Sincerely,
Randy Tonelli

MARTIN 291 POUNDS

Another thing about Doug that I was just thinking about? A few years ago he developed this complete and utter insistence on drinking no beer except from microbreweries. Kind of implying that this was a snobby superiority over the rest of us with our less discriminating palates? But the secret is, I don't think it has anything to do with palates. I don't think he could differentiate Beelzebub's Kill Devil Hills Pale Ale from a can of Schaeffer's if his life depended on it. I think he just likes the funny names. The monks and the werewolves and the lizards and the bug-eyed guys who populate the side of the six-pack box in quirky little pictures. Bad Barney's Bodacious Dark Porter. Sick Pagan Lager. Big Red Fox Cranberry Lambic. Horny Rhino Hoptastic Brew. He finds them entertaining, and the man chooses beer on this basis.

Not just beer, either. Last time he and Cheryl came over for dinner, he brought a bottle of wine with, I swear, a picture of Mothra on the label.

Don't know what made me think of this. Hunger really does have a clarifying effect, I guess. I'm like those wise men who fast, only they gain insight into the nature of the universe, while I gain insight into the nature of Doug. I'm not really fasting as hard as them, so fair enough, I guess.

Only good thing about dieting? We're not drinking real beer anymore. Which means I don't have to hear Doug order anything with a funny waterfowl in its name.

RANDY 281 POUNDS

New rule: I will not masturbate unless I've done at least thirty-five sit-ups.

MARTIN 291 POUNDS

Had the Oscar party at our house. As usual, all of us but Cheryl hadn't seen most of the movies nominated for Oscars this year, but the Oscar party has always been a good excuse to get together and eat. In the past, anyway. This year it was an excuse to get together.

The evening took the same form it always has: An actress shows up on the televised red carpet and Doug would say, "She's hot." (This is how you can tell our wives are there. If we three guys were watching the Oscars by ourselves, which I'm pretty sure we wouldn't, Doug would say "I'd do her" or "I'd do her from behind" or "I'd do her bent over her limo," something along those lines. Then the Oscar statuette itself would get involved.

But our wives are there so he says "She's hot," and Brin rolls her eyes, and Cheryl makes a crack about fake breasts or fake lips, and Dierdre giggles. Every time, she giggles. Which ought to get annoying. And maybe it does—sometimes I think we've all spent too much time together to even know whether we're annoying or not.)

Another starlet in a backless dress: "She's hot."

Brin says, "She's too skinny."

"Not too skinny to be hot," Doug fires back, a little too aggressively I think.

"She is pretty skinny," Randy says, as if it had only just occurred to him that Hollywood actresses are skinny.

"The camera adds ten pounds," Brin says. "In person she must look like a prison-camp victim."

"A hot prison-camp victim, though," Doug says. He shot a contemptuous look over at Randy, who was watching the potato-chip commercial with naked desire. "Like you'd kick her out of bed, Randy."

"I wouldn't kick anyone," Randy said, his eyes glued to the TV screen. "I don't kick. A camera adds ten pounds?"

"Yeah, you didn't know that?" Cheryl said. "That's why Doug looks so big—he's carrying around a bunch of cameras."

Then Dierdre said, apropos of nothing (Dierdre's usually apropos of nothing; she's generally apropos-free), "You think if we were all adults in the '70s we'd swap? Like, swap husbands and wives? Didn't everyone in the '70s do that? With those, what were they, key parties and stuff?"

"I don't think everyone in the '70s did it, Dierdre," Cheryl said. "I don't think it was like a statute."

"If it were a requirement," Brin said, "we'd definitely have to expand our circle of friends."

"Yes, we surely would," Doug said—again, too quickly, and with (I swear) a curled lip. The TV cut back to the red carpet. "She's hot," he said.

Then an actor in a tuxedo wearing a string instead of a tie stepped onto the red carpet and Cheryl said, "Ugh, he's gotten really fat."

"Hey," Doug said, "he is an amazing actor. Give him a break."

"I guess it was different back then," Dierdre said, still

on this other thing. "In the '70s. I mean, everyone was less attractive back then anyway."

No one argued with that.

"And fatter," Randy said.

"People weren't fatter in the '70s," Brin said.

"I wasn't," I say, trying to contribute something.

"No, *you* weren't," Doug said. "But people people were."

"The attractive people were fatter," Dierdre said.

"Except for Twiggy," Cheryl said.

"That would be weird," Randy said. "To be grown-ups in the '70s."

"The lapels alone," I said.

"It would be kind of odd to be called Twiggy and then get fat," said Brin. "You could get in trouble for misrepresenting."

"Or for excessive irony," Cheryl said.

"I'm glad I live in modern times instead of the '70s," Randy said.

"Yeah," Doug said, rubbing his forehead with the heels of his palms. "It's a fucking carnival."

RANDY 280 POUNDS

Okay, twenty-five sit-ups.

DOUG 288 POUNDS

More orange goddamn barrels. Orange barrels since the goddamn Kentucky border. The Tom Clancy book on tape I picked up at the rest stop turned out to have three copies of sides one and two, which I didn't realize until I was searching for side three. And the only radio station I'm getting has friggin' *Prairie Home Companion,* which I've hated ever since that one girl I was dating forced me to listen to that Luke Wobegon bullshit back in college. Had to stop everything to listen to fiddle shit and fake biscuit commercials that didn't even have punch lines. Things I did to get laid back then. What I really wanted to do was tie her down and make her listen to my old Cheech and Chong albums or watch *Blazing Saddles* like seventeen times. That would've knocked that winsome shit right out of her.

Cheryl appreciates good comedy. Something to be said for that. We go to every Farrelly brothers movie. Unwritten rule.

But *Prairie Home Companion* is the only thing I'm getting and the orange barrels are turning me into a zombie and I WANT A FILET-O-FISH SO BAD I COULD SCREAM.

In fact, I *am* screaming. I'm doing seventy-five through orange barrel hell screaming "I WANT A FILET-O-FISH" trying to drown out Garrison fucking wabble voice

Keillor singing some old-timey shit about love and the moon and something that the static seems to deliberately block on every verse. It's a few minutes to two and when I'm done screaming I start hoping that the show is actually going to end at two. I think it's only an hour—God, I hope it's only an hour—and as long as it didn't start at one thirty there's a chance that this part of the nightmare will be over. Won't help me with the Filet-O-Fish or the barrels, but at least it's something.

I could have stayed the night. I had the room until the morning and the company was paying for it. But I just had to get out of there. Had to.

See, trade shows are my thing. I know how to work trade shows. I love sizing up the convention center, getting a handle on what's where and how to get from the exhibit floor to the work sessions to the conference rooms to the convention hotel. I love the move in and the setup of the booth. I've got the setup down to two hours, but I usually take my time, take a couple of breaks to wander the floor, look like I'm doing something important, and scope out the women. I love the few minutes before the doors open and the attendees flood in like water through a busted dam. I love that I know how to get people in the booth, never looking too eager and never, never dipping into desperation. I love having the good golf shirts behind the table to give to special customers and I love when I can offer a free lunch to someone who has been steadily writing orders with me. I love having an excuse to approach women I don't know, check out their badges (conveniently located atop their boobs), learn whether or not they are alone, and make loose plans to see them later—plans that I can break if something better comes along. I love that something better usually comes along.

Because trade show women are away from home just like the guys are. And they're trying to prove that they can hang with the old boy network. So they drink. So they flirt. So they drink some more. So they like when you get a little sensitive at the bar and tell them a little about your weaknesses. They like it when you sort of make a dinner date with them without really making a dinner date (or did you?). Or they like getting an invite to a party they didn't know about because they like to say to their coworkers that they got on the invite list to the party that none of them know about but is *the* party of the event—the one that has, like KC and the Sunshine Band or Tavares playing and where there's an open bar and food catered by the best restaurant in whateverthehell town you are in.

If they are rooming with someone, they like when you slip in a mention that you aren't—that you don't understand why your company wastes money on such a big room for one guy. If they are in a single, they like to subtly let you know that they aren't married and when you get back to your room or to her room, they like that you have something to drink or they like to show you that they have something to drink. They usually make it a point, in between too-aggressive kisses, that they've never done anything like this and you promise them you won't tell and they usually take off their own shirts and they usually really dig it when you go down on them and they usually are surprised that after you've released that you take the time to take them there, too.

And they always leave before you wake up. Even if it's her room.

This time, though, nothing.

Nothing.

There were five prime targets during setup. Another two once the doors opened. Had lunch with one. Invited two to the party. Dined alone but ran into one at the bar and told her about the gig.

At the party, none of them showed, but that happens. Business commitments and all that. But the two prospects there, drunk as they were, dodged like it was a contest and, shit, it's been six, maybe seven years since I've gone back to my room alone on the night of this trade show. The Expo gods were playing some kind of fucking joke.

Or . . . and here's the really scary part that I've been trying to shake from my mind since I checked out (chick at the desk wouldn't even tell me what time she was off): They don't like the new me. The thinner me.

I know. I know. It makes no sense. Why would losing nineteen pounds scare away an entire class of women? But what else could it be? The variable has been isolated. I remember very clearly this same show last year when I had a choice—a choice—between two blonds at the bar *before* the party. If I wasn't obligated, I could have blown off the whole thing, romped with one, met the other for late drinks and had a double header. Fat guy had no problem, man breasts and all.

Two years ago at this show, it was a redhead no more

than twenty-two who hung around the booth almost the whole day like some kind of groupie. Three years. Four years. There was someone going all the way back to year one, when I banged a maintenance woman, a fact that I'm not proud of but, come on, I was still kind of ramping up.

Orange barrels.

And another exit and another sign giving me my Burger King, McD's, KFC choices. Used to stop at least twice on every road trip.

I want a Filet-O-Fish.

Haven't had one in six months.

That's wrong.

If I pulled off now, I'd have a Filet-O-Fish, large fry, big Coke. Not too much ice. Extra tartar sauce on the sandwich. Extra salt on the fries. Handful of fries at a time.

Orange barrels.

Blazing Saddles is a funny goddamn movie.

The static has taken over *A Prairie Home Companion*. It's past two and I don't know if it's over or not. I hit the scan button searching for whatever.

On the fourteenth I leave for another trade show in Harrisburg.

If nothing happens in Harrisburg, I've got some serious decision making to do.

To: Doug@linklink.com, MBB@yahoo.com
From: Randy12479@aol.com
Subject: Quick questions

Guess which two guys won't be getting oral pleasure from
our hooker friend?
  You guessed it: Doug and Martin.
  That's because I won the side bet.
  Suckers . . . I mean, suck-less-ers.

—Randy

"Winners can't be losers."

To: MBB@yahoo.com
From: Doug@linklink.com
Subject: Thanks to Randy,

I may never enjoy oral sex again.
  My life is shit.

—Doug

Doug E. Garrison, Sales Manager
T.H.E. Solutions, "Better people through business"
One Park Plaza

***This e-mail is the property of T.H.E. Solutions and is subject
to scrutiny accordingly. This account is strictly for professional
use only.***

RANDY 278 POUNDS

Okay, that was awkward.

I did my twenty sit-ups, and this of course entitled me to my reward.

Then Ty came into the bedroom.

I thought he was all caught up in his computer game; I should've been safe for hours. When I played the game it took me forever to get the bronze monkey or whatever the thing was. In fact I never did get it. But these kids, they're better at these things than we are. Generational thing.

So he walked into the bedroom. I was dressed and everything, wearing my sweatpants, but still I'm sure it looked suspicious. Since I was on the bed I told him I was napping and having a violent nightmare. Actually, I've used that before.

PRO: Ty doesn't think his dad is an obsessed pervert.
CON: Ty thinks his dad's a psycho who has violent nightmares all the time.

He'll be masturbating before long, if he isn't already. After that the jig is up, though we'll probably all choose to maintain the fiction for comfort's sake. "Ty, what are you doing in that bathroom for so long?" "Having a violent nightmare, Dad!"

Seems convenient.

Just as well, it wasn't going well. I was torn between thinking about Dierdre, thinking about Brin's prostitute friend, or thinking about my old standby, the young Suzanne Somers. For some reason none of them was really doing it for me, and my mind kept going back to this image of that wrinkly old waitress at Pibb's standing over my table with a huge plate of loaded potato skins. That was hot.

But not hot enough. Even before Ty walked in I knew I wasn't going to get the bronze monkey.

DOUG 282 POUNDS

They say that the best way to lose weight is to make sure people know you're trying to lose weight. I have issues with this, partly because I don't feel like giving other people the right to look at me funny when I feel like eating a doughnut, and partly because I expect telling a bunch of people to watch out for my weight would just encourage me to treat the whole fucking thing like a game. The more people who know I'm not supposed to be eating dough-nuts, then the more I'd be trying to eat doughnuts when they're not around. Sneaking one into my jacket pocket and then shoving the thing into my mouth as soon as the elevator doors close. Leaning under the table during a meeting to get something out of my briefcase, and taking a few bites. Seriously, I'd be eating twice as much as I ever was. Not because I really wanted the fucking doughnuts—though their charms are self-evident—but because I wanted to make everyone else look like chumps. I'd be much more motivated by that than by hunger or greed or food. "Sonsabitches, you all were watching to make sure I didn't gain weight, and I gained *eight pounds*! *Now* who's the asshole?"

The people who make up strategies for weight loss don't think about stuff like that. Or about people like me.

But way more people know that I'm losing weight—

and why I'm doing it—than I'm happy with anyway. So I guess I'm following that rule.

The other thing you're supposed to do is exercise with a partner. Because when a friend's expecting you it's supposedly harder to wuss out than when you're doing it alone. Again, these people vastly underestimate how comfortable I feel screwing over my friends. Still, I hate that goddamn gym so much that I thought, "Why not?" Plus, it's finally nice outside again. So I asked Randy if he wanted to go running with me. I chose Randy because he's doing so well with this weight-loss shit—fucking ex-athletes—I figured maybe some of his metabolic karma could rub off on me. Besides, there's that thing where Martin always thinks he's more interesting than I am, and when I'm already miserable I don't need that.

So we got together in our workout clothes. It was awkward. Standing there together, making small talk, staring out into space as if we could see the horizon and were inspecting it for clues as to how this run was going to go. Then silence. Then Randy started stretching, and I kinda got the feeling that he doesn't usually stretch before running but it's something you're supposed to do so now that there's a witness he'd better do it. So I started stretching, like that was what I was just about to do anyway. Made me feel like an asshole.

Then we started running. Randy goes faster than me, which was the first issue. He had to slow down for my benefit, like I was the virgin and he was the pro indulging my clumsy ineptitude. Then he started talking.

Jesus, he wants to talk! I started to really, really miss John Adams.

"Where'd you hear that, about how you're supposed to exercise with someone?" he asked me.

"In a book," I said. Like monosyllables would conserve my energy.

"Like a book you bought, or a book you were just browsing through?"

"Book a friend had. Guy at work."

"Did he know you were trying to lose weight?" he said.

"No. Just had it." Trying to think of ways to minimize the number of words I said was now taking up more energy than talking would have. Like I was composing telegrams. Telegrams to Randyland. "Looked through it. When he wasn't looking."

"I told everyone at work I was losing weight," Randy said. "They've been all supportive and stuff. Guys on the team are really rooting for me. 'Lookin' good, coach,' that kind of thing."

"Great."

"Was it a good book? What was the title of the book?"

I muttered "I don't know," only without the consonants.

Some people passed us. Randy said, "You think people see us running together and think we're, like, boyfriend and boyfriend?"

At this point Randy looked behind him to see that I'd stopped running. He stopped, too.

"You tired?" he asked me. "You look mad. Are you tired, or just mad?"

We decided to stop running together and went instead

to Barnes & Noble to look at their weight-loss books. We both made a huge point, silently, of not getting a Frappuccino from the coffee shop there. Made a point of not even looking in the direction of the coffee shop. Didn't say anything, but we each noticed, because what's the point of being so virtuous otherwise?

Randy sat on the floor in the aisle flipping through books after I finished looking through them. *Weight Loss for Morons, Exercise for Cretins, Heart Healthy Cooking for Retardos.* The target audience for publishers these days is people who can barely read.

"There are so many books," Randy said.

"It's like a fucking religion, this shit," I said. "When we're done we should write a book."

"Yeah, yeah. *Weight Loss for Perverts.*"

"*Better Cardio Through Prostitution,*" I said, "*for Loser Shit-for-Brains.*"

Randy was laughing so hard he pounded Dr. Atkins on the carpeted floor facedown. "We'll sell a million!"

We read some more. I was a little self-conscious. Two sorta fat guys reading together in the diet and exercise section. But it's not as embarrassing as being seen in the self-help sex book section. (Which, for the record, isn't worth it, because most of those books aren't even sexy. You'll find better boner material in the Art/Photography section, or the Women's Interest row of the magazine rack. Just so you know.)

Randy looked up. "How good of friends were Brin and this woman in college, you think?"

"I really don't know, Randy," I said. "The things I don't

know about Brin could have filled my preexercise ass."
Why don't I know more about my friends' wives, anyway? Oh, yeah, that's right: I don't give a shit. Knowing
stuff about my own wife is work enough, for Christ's
sake.

"Just seems weird," said Randy. "You'd think if they
were that good of friends Brin would have said something to Martin, like 'Wow, this friend of mine became a
prostitute.' And then you'd think Martin would have said
something to us, because, well, that's way more interesting than most of the things we say to each other."

"They probably weren't that good of friends," I said.
"Just good enough for Brin to be able to call her and be
like, 'Here's a ridiculous idea.'"

Randy nodded and opened a book on yoga. "I kind of
wish we could talk to her ourselves, like get in touch
with her."

"Check out the merchandise, you mean? Make sure
she's not fat from the waist down or something?"

"No, no. I'm sure she has to be, you know, for her job
and stuff. Just . . ." Randy does this thing where he
searches for words, and then when he finally finds them
they're completely ordinary words. He needs more of
those calendars. ". . . like, to be like, 'What's up? We're the
guys.' I bet there's some way we could track her down.
Some smart, sneaky Jim Rockford thing we could pull off."

"Probably best we don't," I said.

"Maybe not," Randy said. "Isn't yoga what, like,
Gandhi did?"

"Do I look like I know what Gandhi did?"

By now the row was a mess, the floor littered with paperbacks like soldiers at Gettysburg. Randy shook his head. "There are so many of these books," he said again.

"It's a moneymaking scheme, Randy," I said. "People who can't make themselves exercise and eat right figure if they spend tons of money on books like these, then at least they're doing something."

Randy nodded and was silent for a long time. Then he said, "We should definitely buy some of these books."

I agreed.

RANDY 269 POUNDS

I gained a pound. How the hell did I gain a pound?

Okay, I know how I gained a pound. You're only supposed to eat one Slim-Fast bar instead of a meal. I ate three. That's how I gained a pound.

Still, it's not right. How much can three of those things weigh, first of all, and second, stuff that doesn't even taste that great shouldn't make you gain a pound. That should be a rule.

MARTIN 287 POUNDS

I don't think I would have been included in the conversation six months ago. Now, though, nobody seemed to have a problem with me being there. In fact, I was looked to for my opinion.

The question was, under what conditions would it be okay to discriminate against someone based on whatever—age, sex, race, size—anything.

"Well," someone said, "it's okay to deny someone the job of jockey if you're six foot two."

"And to say no to a guy who wants to pole dance at a gentleman's club."

I won't bother quoting anymore, because I'm not sure who said what and it all ran together, but here are some of the things that were said:

No problem discriminating when it comes to talent. A comedy club booker isn't obligated to book someone unfunny, a dance troupe to hire someone with two left feet, and so on. But that all fell under the merit category, not really discrimination.

If a person can't comfortably get down the aisle of a plane, he or she had no business being a stewardess.

A health club could deny employment to someone overweight, someone rationalized, because they needed to send a healthy message.

And it was perfectly okay to factor in looks when it comes to hiring a receptionist or someone else who interfaces with the public.

TV anchors and reporters.

Front of house hotel staff.

Hookers (in Nevada, of course).

Restaurant hostesses. Restaurant waitresses? There was some controversy on this point.

Then someone asked, "What about taxi drivers? No one expects taxi drivers to be good-looking, but they interface with the public." Why is that? One person suggested it was because nobody associated the taxi driver's appearance with his ability to do the job well. I said it was an economics question: Taxis are often scarce resources, and if the driver of the taxi you hail is butt-ugly, he knows you're not going to turn him down for another taxi. (I thought that was pretty smart; I think the others thought so, too.) Monica, who started here around the same year I did, said it was because most taxi drivers are male and males never have to worry about their weight or appearance as much as women do. (This raised the question of why most taxi drivers are male, which we agreed to table until a future bullshit session.)

Then someone said it was because taxi drivers are forced to sit on their asses all day, so we expect them to be heavy, and to have hemorrhoids. That pretty much killed the discussion.

Still, throughout the whole thing no one even gave me a wary glance or a nervous look, like "Is he offended?"

It did make me wonder what would have happened if I'd tried to be an actor or a TV anchor, though. Before. And whether Monica would be making as much as I do (which I think she does) if she were fat.

To: Alumni@cedarcollege.com
From: Randy12479@aol.com
Subject: My call earlier today

Mr. Brunhill,

As we discussed, I am attaching a photo of the woman in question.

As I told you by phone, the photo was included in a small pile of pictures among my late wife's belongings. Given the apparent age of the woman and the fact that my late wife's parents and brother cannot identify her, I assume that she is a friend from college.

Since the other photos were of very important people in her life, I am desperately trying to reach this woman in order to tell her the bad news and to share with her a small piece of the estate (mostly jewelry) that my late wife left behind. At this time of great sorrow, reaching out to these people who were important to my late wife is very important to me.

I welcome any help possible and, once the estate has been sorted out, will happily send a sizable check to the alumni fund.

Go Cedar Wildcats!
Randy Tonelli

"Winning isn't everything, it's the only thing."

------·------·-----·------·------·------·-----·------·------·------·------·------·

To: Alumni@cedarcollege.com
From: Randy12479@aol.com
Subject: My note last week

Mr. Brunhill,

Attached is a copy of the note I sent last week regarding the photo of the (I believe) Cedar College alumnus whose picture was found in my late wife's belongings. As I believe I mentioned, after my wife's car accident, I found the photo of this woman among those of other people important to her life. I very much want to reach this woman and tell her the sad news. Could you please help identify her? I believe she was in the class of 1991.

As it turns out, my wife's estate was even larger than I believed. One good thing that has come of this tragedy is that, once I find this woman, I can get down to the serious business of making even more generous donations to the college than the ones she outlined in her last wishes.

Go Cedar Wildcats!,

Randy Tonelli

"Do or do not, there is no try."—Yoda

To: Alumni@cedarcollege.com
From: Randy12479@aol.com
Subject: The generous donation

Mr. Brunhill,

I believe you misunderstood my note. It was not explicitly written into my late wife's will that a donation be made to the college. It's just that I knew she would have wanted that. However, the tone of your letter—and your insistence on knowing my wife's maiden name—leads me to believe that you are more concerned with scoring a bequest than in helping out the husband of that alumnus find another alumnus who would want to know that she (the first alumnus) has passed away.

At this time of great sensitivity, such action is disturbing indeed. To watch, over the past year, as she withered away from the effects of ALS (known to most people as Lou Gehrig's disease) and then to have a simple request to her beloved institution left unanswered and, in fact, met with suspicion is too much for me to deal with right now.

I once again call on your basic humanity and desire to do the right thing and request the requested information.

Go Wildcats!
Randy Tonelli

"Winning at all costs is still winning."

To: Alumni@cedarcollege.com
From: Randy12479@aol.com
Subject: The car accident

    Mr. Brunhill,

How rude of you to cite what you see as a contradiction. For the record, when I said "car accident" I was referring to the fact that, while she was being rushed to the hospital, the ambulance in which she was riding was struck by a Ford Taurus.

  I think it goes without saying, sir, that this brings to a close any potential transactions we might have together now or in the future. Unless you change your mind and want to answer my question.

Hope the Hanford Warriors
KICK YOUR ASS this year!
Randy Tonelli

"Close only counts in horseshoes and hand grenades."

MARTIN 284 POUNDS

She practically shit herself when she saw me. I mean, her jaw was down to her boobs (which looked pretty sweet, by the way—I wonder if she had work done). It was exactly the reaction I wanted because, no matter how cool Brin has been about things, in the back of my mind I kept anticipating the moment Amy would see me. Brin never knew me when I was a regular-size guy. Amy did. Amy saw me in this body. Amy made love with me in this body. She watched me grow and grow and grow and no matter what happened between us, she never called me fat. She never commented on my slide into obesity. Never said a word as I threw out worthless belts and sent bags of clothes to AmVets. Suffered gladly as I spilled over into her airplane seat.

She just stoically put up with her amazing colossal husband and, I learned later, politely put off the advances of Perfect Guy at the office and then decided not to put off the advances of Perfect Guy at the office and then fell in love with Perfect Guy at the office and then honestly and openly told her husband that she was in love with Perfect Guy and asked what I thought they should do about it.

And I said she should do what she feels she should do and I didn't think that that meant taking the kids away and when she said it meant taking the kids to Ohio where

Perfect Guy was getting transferred I had a moment of doubt. A moment of How Could a Fat Guy Like Me Raise Two Kids Without a Mom and in the interest of staying amicable I let her have the kids as long as I was welcome in their home and I could have them visit for as long as they wanted—with a minimum of six weeks a year—and that there would be some time between when she and the kids moved out and when she told them that she was dating this other guy so that the kids wouldn't wonder what the hell was wrong with Daddy or what did Daddy do that was so wrong that Mommy needed to get away from him and run to someone else.

And I wanted to hear her say that, when the kids get older, they would be able to spend more time with me if they wanted. And she wanted to hear me say that I wouldn't bad-mouth her in front of them or try to get them over to my "side."

At the time, I didn't have a side, so I agreed to everything.

I knew when I saw her after not seeing her for six months that she'd joke about the weight loss somehow and she did. She said, "Who are you and what have you done with my kids' father?" I had to play along and laugh a little and say that her ex-husband got caught in a vice at the local giant tool company and she said that I look great. Really great. And she stared at me for too long, long enough for me to know that tonight with Brin I wouldn't be thinking about the prostitute.

RANDY 274 POUNDS

That's right. I'm shirtless.

It's okay. Men go shirtless all the time. Men who look a lot worse than I'm starting to look, that's for sure. Nothing wrong with it. I'm getting stares. Stares are a good thing. Used to get stares all the time in college, when I used to go shirtless all the time. In the dorm freshman year they used to call me Shirtless Guy. It was good to have a thing. I haven't been a guy with a thing for a long time, thought maybe that just comes with growing up but maybe not, maybe you can still be a grown-up guy with a thing. My thing could be being Shirtless Guy. Or being not that fat. Not That Fat Guy. I could have two things. Oh, but that's greedy.

Getting stares. I think that woman likes what she sees. Waggle my left hand at her: sorry, babe, married. If only. In another lifetime, maybe. But who could blame her? A torso like this torso is starting to look? Oh, maybe she's married too, she's showing me her finger. That's not her ring finger. Anyway.

Feelin' good. Getting attention. Maybe this plan wasn't so bad after all. Maybe I'm glad, maybe it's worth it. Maybe it would be worth it even if there weren't that girl at the end of it. Especially if there weren't that girl at the end of it. But Dierdre seems really invested in the girl thing, so. Keeps describing to me the things I could do with the girl, gets really into it. Said maybe I should videotape it. Which makes me feel weird, I said maybe I could do a few sketches? I found Brin's picture of the girl under Dierdre's side of the bed the other morning. She's really excited about my losing weight.

Yeah, they're lookin'. This woman's looking, for sure, she's looking me up and down. Looking, looking. Now she's pointing. Pointing? A sign. "No Shirts, No Shoes, No Service." Oh. I get it. Yeah, okay, that's cool. I'm fine with that. If everybody could do it all the time, it wouldn't be one of my things.

Still, when did Applebee's get so uptight?

MARTIN 281 POUNDS

I'm sitting in the coffee shop reading the newspaper and trying not to think about whether this coffee I'm drinking is really worth three dollars or not, sitting among all the would-be writers with their laptops and the wannabe investors with their business pages and the wives looking for a little alone time away from their husbands and the husbands sneaking some time away from their wives. Me, I just want to read the paper and the windows are nice here in the morning, and the ridiculous prices they put on those muffins and Krispies Treats are the best thing to happen to weight loss since Richard Simmons.

So this woman walks in. A young woman, midtwenties maybe, kind of girl I've always had kind of a weakness for: the kind who looks way too smart for me. That's always been a pleasant source of superiority for me: my capacity to lust after women I know Doug and Randy are way too shallow to go for. Brin's hot, but what makes me disproportionately proud was never being a fat guy married to a gorgeous wife but being a fat guy married to a woman who's read lots of Virginia Woolf and can win an argument on the Israel-Palestine situation.

So here's this woman, young, shapely, her nice round end swinging in a funky skirt that looks like the kind of clothes overprivileged grad students buy in stores that sell stuff that looks like vintage clothes for full price.

Doug would think her butt's too big, but Doug's full of it. She's wearing an outfit that's very fetching but also looks like the kind of outfit chosen by someone who thinks wearing earth tones constitutes some kind of political statement. She's got big brown eyes and all this brown hair, and when she reaches up to clamp a bunch of that hair at the back of her head with a clip, you can see through her shapeless beige sweater that she's got a nice chest, too.

This is way better than reading the paper.

Then she looks up and our gazes lock. Damn, caught looking, I hate that. Then she smiles. Huge smile. Big, all-encompassing, long-lost-friend smile. Such a delighted and welcoming smile I felt awkward and guilty: She thinks she recognizes me. She's meeting someone she doesn't know and she assumes it's me because I was watching her. I look down: mm, good newspaper. I look up and she smiles again and sets about doing whatever she's doing at her table. It was just a smile. Just an enormous electric dazzling put-the-sun-to-shame smile.

I never get smiles like that unless it's a woman I know (and especially not then, har har). So what is this—I've lost weight, I look better, and now I get smiles? I've lost weight and feel better about myself and present myself differently and now I get the smiles? Or I've gotten the smiles all along but never noticed before because I never expected them?

Whatever the situation is, I definitely need to start drinking more coffee.

To: BrinM@compumail.net
From: Chercher@worknet.com
Subject: RE: RE: The Plan

Hey, buddy. So, wow, I don't know if you've noticed but the fellas have lost a lot of weight. I mean, they've lost a LOT of weight. They could look like three Calista Flockhart impersonators eventually, these guys. I know they have a long way to go but they're looking better, I suspect they're feeling better, improved self-esteem, better health, longer life spans.

Am I alone in feeling this is catastrophic?

And if that weren't enough to keep me up at nights in a cold sweat, this morning I was eating a Danish and Doug looks at me, looking all informed and collaborative, and goes "You know those go straight to your hips."

When did I marry my sister? This is all bad. Mayday! Mayday!

MY DAD
By Ty Tonelli

I picked my dad to write about for this essay.

My dad is named Randolph but everyone calls him Randy. When I was little and found out his long name was Randolph, I got mixed up and thought it was Rudolph, like the red-nosed reindeer. Speaking of Christmas, you might know my dad because he played Santa Claus once at a mall. Maybe you sat on his lap.

My dad doesn't have an interesting job and isn't famous, but he did do something really cool. He lost lots of weight. We were in the store last week and he kept handing me packages of hamburger meat and he put more and more and more of them in my arms and then he said that that was how much weight he lost. It was really heavy. I dropped some of them and people were looking at us funny but my dad does stuff all the time that makes people look at us funny. He's a good dad and a sometimes emberesing dad.

I'm not emberessed about the weight thing, though. He told me that he was doing it because he wanted to live a long time and watch me grow up. He said if I'm going to be a major-league baseball player I'm going to need a healthy dad to help him practice. My mom likes that he is losing weight but pretty soon I think she's going to be heavier than him and that might make her mad.

My dad is the hero that I chose to write about and I think I picked a good one. People can learn from what my dad did. You don't need a reason to get in shape. Even a fat guy can do it.

MARTIN 278 POUNDS

We were rooting around in the kitchen looking for something we were allowed to eat before watching the movie. It's not like any of our kitchens have stuff we aren't allowed to eat anymore—I can't remember the last time Randy or Doug or I risked coming across a bag of Cheetos or frozen macaroni and cheese in our own homes by accident. Still, what you find has to be edible, and appetizing, and that means finding something other than baking soda, or coffee beans, or a can of Tab.

And out of nowhere Randy goes, "You guys ever go shirtless?"

Like he's asking about a lifestyle choice. Doug, ever the voice of reason, says, "What the fuck are you talking about, Randy?"

"Like, in public. We can do that, you know," Randy said. "Women can't but we can. Go shirtless. And we're, the three of us, probably, getting to the point where maybe we wouldn't mind."

"You can't go shirtless just anywhere, Randy," I said.

"Yeah, no, apparently not. But still."

This line of inquiry drowned in the pool of silence it deserved. But then Doug goes, "How you guys lookin'? With your shirts off?"

"Good!" Randy said, a little too eagerly.

"Fine," I said. "I've lost some weight."

Doug had this little-boy grin he gets sometimes. "You guys want to compare?"

"What, like on a scale?" I asked.

"Naw. Just lift our shirts," Doug said. "See how we're all doing. A motivational thing."

"Okay!" Randy said. I bet he was one of those little kids who runs around naked until they're eight.

"You guys are queer," I said, as though reverting to grade-school insults were the only way to smack these two down. I had a sense that I'd been struggling with the weight-loss challenge more than them and didn't care to have that confirmed visually.

"Seriously, though, guys, haven't you pretty much been more conscious of your bodies over the past few months than you ever have before?" Randy asked. "Like, how you look, and how it feels? How you feel or look in these jeans, or whether this shirt makes you look or feel fat?"

"I guess," I said.

"Yeah," Doug said.

And then, because Randy always has to say out loud the thing everyone else is avoiding saying out loud, Randy said, "Makes me realize what it must be like to be a woman. And stuff."

"What?" Doug said.

"No . . ." I said.

"Because women, they're always, and now we—" Randy continued.

"You saying we're womanly?" Doug asked, not as a threat but genuinely curious.

"No . . ." Randy said.

"Or feminine?"

"No!"

"Women think about their bodies and their food and clothes and stuff but when we do it, we do it in a totally masculine way," Doug said.

"It's inherently masculine," I said. "Definitively masculine." Using words I knew Randy would respect.

"First of all, we're only doing it to bone a woman . . ." Doug continued.

"But isn't that why women are body conscious?" Randy asked. "To attract sexual partners, and stuff?"

Doug looked a little panicked. "There's no way women would lift their shirts in a kitchen to compare how they're all doing."

"Let's do it!" I said.

We all lifted our shirts. Doug looked a little better than I expected, Randy a little worse. But we were all doing okay. We were all also realizing that the next step in this exercise would be to scrutinize and comment on one another's abdomens. Nobody wanted to do that. So we all dropped the shirts and went back to foraging.

"That was masculine," Doug said, just to confirm it. "It's like when you're a bunch of teenaged guys and you all compare penises, see whose is the biggest."

"Yeah," Randy said, though I think he was thinking the same thing I was, which was: You did that?

There was a silence, and then Doug said, "Hey, you guys wanna—?"

"No, Doug."

RANDY 269 POUNDS

Okay, so Martin didn't look like he was doing that great when we shirt-lifted. But that other thing we did later, when the DVD got boring? The man measures up.

DOUG 281 POUNDS

Was lying awake in bed, fantasizing nostalgically about chocolate milk, when it hit me: If only the girls had imposed a fucking deadline! "You have to drop the weight within this time limit in order to collect the prize." That would have made everything soooooo much fucking easier: lose weight for a while, look like sleeping with this hooker is something I desperately want to do, and then when I haven't hit the target weight by the deadline, nobody's the wiser. I could lose the game without looking like I lost the game.

Plus, then this hungry hell I now call my life would have been finite. I could have seen my way to the end of it. Instead, things could go on like this for decades.

Why didn't they give us a deadline? That would have made sense. Not like I can say anything now, though. Not having a deadline is allegedly better for me. If I allegedly want to sleep with this hooker, which I allegedly want to do, why in the world would I call attention to the fact that the women made the major boneheaded mistake of not giving us a deadline?

Fuck!

Women, they're not strategic. Enough. Used to think that was something I liked about them.

So I'm at Pibb's with Randy after work; we've met up to punish ourselves with low-calorie low-carb light beerlike substances, I'm looking at Randy watching the TV over the bar and thinking the only thing I envy about Randy is the fact that he doesn't have to wear a tie to work most days; hell, he doesn't even have to wear real pants.

Also the tight curve of Dierdre's ass, I guess I envy that a little too, but consider what that ass is attached to and the fact that the whole package is usually wrapped in outfits that feature bunnies or Christmas trees and that envy gets pretty flaccid pretty quick.

So I say to Randy, "Boy, good thing they didn't give us a deadline, huh?"

Randy blinks. "Huh?"

"The girls. Brin and the others. Good thing they didn't impose a deadline, huh? Like, 'If you don't lose the weight by this date, you can't have the sex.'"

Randy nodded thoughtfully. "Yeah, yeah, I guess," he said. "Good thing they didn't say that, or we might not get to. Have the sex."

"It would be considerably less likely," I said. "We would be considerably less likely to sleep with Brin's prostitute friend."

"Yeah," Randy said. "Yeah." Then: "Which would be too bad. Because we want to sleep with her."

"Yes, we do," I said. "Which is why I'm saying: Good thing they didn't give us a deadline."

"Good thing," Randy agreed. "Because then we'd be really disappointed."

"Yep," I said. "Yep yep."

Dumbass Randy. Should've known I couldn't count on him to be on my side.

MARTIN 272 POUNDS

One of those books that Randy and Doug gave me—and, side issue, by the way, when did Randy and Doug become book buddies? All of a sudden they're the literate ones? Because that means I'm seriously slipping, makes me feel like I need to dig out some Thoreau or one of the other books in the boxes in the attic that were assigned in college but rarely read—anyway, one of those books suggests all these ways to exercise at work, just changes to your daily routine that are supposed to make you healthier without your even noticing it. Some of these ideas are ridiculous. Like all these muscle things you're supposed to do while you're sitting at your desk. Ab crunches. Arm flexing. Butt clenching. Supposed to tone you up and no one will even notice. Except the first time I tried, Monica from purchasing stopped in my office and said "There's some concern out here, Martin—are you shitting your pants?"

Much merriment followed. But it wouldn't have been very funny if I had been shitting my pants, thanks very much.

One of the few things in the book that makes sense is its recommendation that you stop taking the elevator. Just stop, period. Pretend the elevator's never been invented. Just take the stairs. Makes sense, sounds good, and there's a lot about it I like. I like it that it implicitly encourages you to feel superior to everyone else who does take the elevator. I already did that, but only to people who used the elevator to go up or down fewer than two floors. Now I can be judgmental about virtually everyone else.

I also like it because I like to think I'm not a particularly uptight or germophobic person, but cramming into an elevator with a bunch of other people is the one daily practice that always made me feel like wrapping myself in plastic.

What the book doesn't mention is that this new practice will actually have a pretty significant effect on your daily schedule. Especially if you work on a sort of high-up floor. I actually leave for work a little bit earlier in the morning to allow for the fact that I'm taking the stairs. But on the plus side, it also gives you all this time to think about stuff. Yesterday by the time I reached my floor I had managed to remember the quadratic equation, which I couldn't do at all back on the ground floor. Tomorrow maybe I'll mull over America's role in the United Nations.

The book also doesn't mention how desolate and bleak office building stairwells are. You can tell they pretty much expect everyone to be taking the elevators, because the stairwells look like they were designed to look like Rikers Island. At first I kept flashing back to the cinder-block stairwell in my freshman dorm where one Friday night someone vomited on a landing and no one cleaned it up until Monday morning. This can all be a little grim, but also—glass half full, here—kind of bracing, because you feel like you have a better understanding of this building than everyone else does. All they know is the wall-to-wall carpeting and the bland public art and the windows. We stairwell dwellers, we have the whole picture.

And there are other stairwell dwellers. I'd assumed I would be the only one who ever used the stairs, but there's a whole subculture here. The woman in the short skirts who looks like she weighs about seventy pounds and takes the stairs with such urgency that I'm pretty sure she not only read the same book I did but has incorporated it into her whole eating-disorder lifestyle. The big guy in glasses who just stands on the fifth-floor landing, just stands there, I'm pretty sure because it's the only place he can go for long stretches of time where no one else in his department can find him. We nod at each other every day when I pass; sometimes we say "Hey." My unspoken subtext: "Your secret's safe with me, pal." His: "Thanks, buddy. Good luck with the weight loss."

Not people I'd invite over to my house on the weekend, but it's nice to know if I collapsed on the stairwell some day, someone would find me before days went by.

BRIN

Okay. I've called this emergency meeting because we have a crisis. Everyone knows we have a crisis, that's why we're all here. Dierdre, you look like you don't know we have a crisis. You know what the crisis is, yeah? What? No, no no. No. Why, what's wrong with my hair? No, it's not that.

The guys, as Cheryl has observed repeatedly and ad nauseam, are losing weight, a lot of weight. They're losing weight with a vengeance. It's looking maybe like there's the slightest chance they're going to hit their target and then some. Just keep on going. Wasting away like Camille, these fellas. Dropping pounds right and left.

Yes.

Right.

Dierdre, why are you smiling?

You're smiling and nodding.

This isn't appropriate crisis behavior. Look at Cheryl, you should look like her. Anxious and sort of crampy. That's the place we're in here. Try it, show me. Try "worried." Can you do "vexed"? Never mind.

No, of course we wanted them to lose weight. Of course that's why we did all this in the first place. Obviously. Yes, we're succeeding. Hooray for us. But there's the little matter of the reward we promised them. The trophy at the end of the race. I mean, honestly, I told Martin we set the goal where we did because we wanted to be ambitious, because that was just how serious his health situation was. He had no idea it was because I figured that was a weight he'd never be able to reach in a million years.

Shows what I know.

Cheryl, don't look at me like that.

So this motivation, I guess it was even more motivating than I expected. Yet again I've underestimated the male appetite for poontang.

Come off it, Dierdre, I know you know that word.

For some reason I had insufficient faith in the same masculine drive that keeps *Maxim* magazine in business and gives Pamela Anderson a long, healthy career. Why I thought it would be limited in its capacity to keep our husbands away from onion rings is, in retrospect, beyond me. It's possible that I'm a complete idiot.

Now you're both smiling and nodding. I swear I don't need this right now.

What's that? No, Dierdre, of course we all knew what we were getting into. We knew what we were promising. It's not that I'm so upset by the idea of letting Martin sleep with another woman. I'm actually surprised by how well I can bring myself around to that idea. The trade-off is more than worth it. In fact, I'm completely okay with the idea of letting Martin sleep with this other woman.

It's just, it would be a lot less problematic if this other woman actually existed.

Dierdre? Dierdre?

See, yeah, *that's* the facial expression I was thinking you should have.

To: BrinM@compumail.net
From: Chercher@worknet.com
Subject: RE: Oops

I swear I thought she knew, too.

DOUG 270 POUNDS

Cheryl and I are eating our low-calorie dinner at the table in the kitchen in stony silence. We used to have the TV on when we ate dinner, the news or *Jeopardy!* or whatever. Then we had some kind of conversation in which I guess we agreed that it was a bad thing for a marriage if the married people ate in front of the TV every night, not talking to each other. Not very civilized, or healthy, I forget. So we turned the TV off, and now we eat without the TV, not talking to each other. Yeah, we're way healthy.

Because speaking would, however, be preferable to eating another steamed carrot, I looked over at Cheryl and said "So, I was just saying to Randy the other day, good thing you girls didn't give us a deadline."

Cheryl was chewing. "What?"

"Good thing you didn't impose a deadline," I said. "Otherwise it would've been harder for us to collect the reward. Sleep with that chick, you know. Lucky for us you guys didn't do that."

Cheryl nodded slowly. "Lucky for you," she said.

God, am I ever looking forward to my trip on the twenty-second. I'm going to eat in front of the hotel TV like a fucking savage.

To: BrinM@compumail.net
From: Chercher@worknet.com
Subject: We're IDIOTS!

WE SHOULD HAVE IMPOSED A DEADLINE!!!!!!

DOUG 269 POUNDS

So I know if I hit 210 I have to sleep with Brin's friend. But what if I keep losing? At some point do I win a whole passel of concubines? This could be worth it after all.

CHERYL

Doug,

Please do what you can to get out of the trip on the 22–24. I'd really like to do something for our anniversary, even if it's just dinner and a movie. And I won't give you a hard time if you order a cheeseburger. And it's okay if it's an action movie as long as it doesn't have Vin Diesel in it.

—C

MARTIN 272 POUNDS

Standing in front of the mirror with my shirt off this morning I allowed myself to enjoy the possibly deluded conviction that I look better than I used to. I tried different poses, different angles. I froze in midstride waving to see how I might look just walking down the street waving at someone (if I were doing that wearing nothing but my pajama bottoms). Yeah, no matter what I tried, I looked pretty good.

Brin says that when a woman looks in a mirror, even a great-looking woman, all she sees are the flaws. And when a guy looks in the mirror, even a totally dumpy guy, all he sees are the good things.

Another reason to be happy I'm a guy.

Another pose. Looks good. Pose. Good again.

Then I tried dancing.

Big mistake.

DOUG 268 POUNDS

She let me pick the movie. She let me put butter on the popcorn. She let me hold the popcorn so that I didn't have to reach over to her every time I wanted some.

We went out for burgers afterward. We talked about nothing particularly important. We came home. We had sex. We both came. We both fell asleep.

Damned if I can figure it out, but it was really a nice anniversary.

MARTIN 271 POUNDS

Going out with your friends can be a lot of work in the best of circumstances. Going to a movie, for instance, with Brin and Doug and Randy and Cheryl and Dierdre? Good luck finding one that all six of us wouldn't mind seeing but haven't seen already. Good luck dealing with the situation afterward, when Cheryl's making fun of everything that happened in the movie and Dierdre's calling everything that happened in the movie "cute." If we took Dierdre to a David Cronenberg movie she'd find something she could call "cute."

(That was a pretty clever pop culture reference, if I do say so myself, though its impact was probably mitigated by the fact that I had to get on the Internet and look around before I remembered David Cronenberg's name as the guy who directed *Scanners,* a movie about people who could blow each other's heads up. I'd use the line in conversation except that no one I know would probably get it, except Brin. Maybe Cheryl.)

It's even harder to find something to do as a group now that eating has become this sore subject. Sure, all the chain restaurants have heart-healthy and dietary entrées that they signify on their menus with little red hearts, but that doesn't help fix the fact that in this particular group of friends, healthy eating has gotten completely entwined with guilt, bullying, and extramarital sex. They might as well dot the menus with little penises. "I'll have the penis-healthy chicken wrap."

So we went to this club, which was a terrible idea but at least it was terrible for all the most innocuous reasons: because we're not clubby people, because we're getting older and don't like to be reminded of it, because Dierdre doesn't own any black clothes, because the loud music hurts Brin's ears, because none of us are dancers.

But at least it doesn't have anything to do with weight loss. Or, as far as I know, prostitutes.

It's a new club that opened in town, pretty hip and youthful for this particular midwestern burg. In fact, someone said they saw on the crawl along the bottom of CNN's screen that this was one of the first oxygen bars to open in Indiana. Meaning, apparently, you can go up to the bar and buy some oxygen?

"Doesn't that make you feel like you're in a hospital?" Cheryl said as we filed inside, paying the cover charge two by two.

"I'm not against oxygen or anything," Brin said, "but if I'm going to pay good money for gases, I think I'd prefer something less pedestrian."

"Ooh! Like helium!" Dierdre said.

"Yeah! I'd totally pay for helium," Randy said.

"Right about now I could go for some good carbon monoxide," Doug said.

So we sat around on uncomfortable upholstered ottomans, each of us holding a drink the color of a

Dr. Seuss character, and made conversation. Which used to seem to be more fun than it is now. Seemed more fun in theory, anyway.

Randy broke a lull in the conversation by saying, "Doug and I were talking awhile ago. Saying it sure was a good thing for us that you girls didn't impose a deadline on the—you know. On the thing."

"Yes," Brin said. "Good thing for you guys that we didn't think of that."

"Good for us," Doug said. "Lucky us. Too bad for you."

"Yeah," Dierdre said. "Because that would have solved all kinds of problems. If there were problems, I mean, which there aren't."

I'm really not into this conversation. I'm thinking about going back to the bar or off to the restroom, and taking the scenic route. But then there's always the chance that Dierdre and Cheryl will run off to the restroom, too, and Doug and Randy have made it clear that they feel awkward being left alone with Brin to make conversation. "No offense to your wife, bro," Doug had said, "but I just fucking hate talking to her." No offense taken, I reckon. Reflects poorly on him, frankly.

"I suppose," Brin said, "if we now suggested that we impose a deadline on the deal, you guys would object, because it wasn't part of the previously agreed-upon conditions."

"I suppose we'd have to," Doug said.

"You'd be well within your rights to object," Cheryl said.

"Then," Randy said, "I guess we have no choice but to. Object."

"So you object?" Brin asked.

"You're going to force us to object? Formally?" Doug said.

"Well, you don't have to wear a tie or anything," Cheryl said.

"But you're going to make me say it out loud," Doug said.

"Sure. Why don't you say it out loud," Cheryl said.

"I think it's best if we're all on the same page," Brin said.

"Then yes," Doug said.

"Yes what?" Cheryl said.

"Yes we fucking object, don't try to force your stupid fucking deadline on us now, we know a good thing when we see it," Doug exploded, sloshing his drink all over his sleeve. "These drinks taste like fucking Jolly Ranchers!"

Good times.

RANDY 260 POUNDS

Okay, the whole exercise/weight-loss industry is really confusing. I went out to get some weights. Just some little hand weights that I could work with at home, to complement my sit-ups and so forth. (And I've been doing so many sit-ups since I made a certain little deal with myself that I can't imagine what I might do with weights.) And I went to Target. Because that's where I go for everything when I need to buy something, unless I'm shopping for something superspecialized like drywall screws or, you know, oranges.

And I'm standing in the Target aisle and they have these little blue weights and these things with Velcro you can wrap around your wrists or ankles, almost kind of kinky, and I thought: Wait a minute. These look fine to me, but I'm all serious about my working out, it doesn't seem quite right to buy stuff like this at Target, I should go to a specialty store where people who take this seriously shop.

So I went to the store in the mall called the Health Center. Now, I'm not naive about this industry, I've worked in athletics since I graduated from college. But I'm also no scientist, and I can't figure out

1. *Why almost everything in the so-called Health Center is designed to make you* gain *weight, and*

2. *Why ingesting what looks to me like a bunch of sand would have anything to do with giving you the kind of ripped abs that are pictured on the label on the tub of sand. Also*
3. *Why everything's so expensive.*

The salesman came over and asked if he could help me, but he was so muscly and aggressive I got the feeling he sort of wanted to wrassle.

I went back to Target. Everyone else is fat there. It's kind of nice.

DOUG 265 POUNDS

That bitch.

I married a conniving weasel. How is it I didn't know this?

Is there no such thing as trust? Mutual respect? My God. This woman.

In the first place, the meat on this sandwich is not tofurkey. I'm not an idiot. It's plainly real genuine turkey. And did she think I wouldn't notice the slab of cheese she's laid on here? Fat and empty calories. This is why I like to do all the cooking.

I was immediately suspicious when I saw that there was a sandwich spread but I figured well, okay, that's fine, she's probably trying out some nonfat mayonnaise, maybe it'll be good. But I could swear this is Crisco. She spread Crisco on my fucking sandwich?

Can't look too obvious about sniffing it, she'll notice. Look at her there, sitting, smiling. Reading *Cooking Light* magazine? That's a laugh. I'll bet this is Wonder bread. It congeals suspiciously to the touch.

This is definitely Crisco. And what's this buried under a lettuce leaf in my salad? A chunk of bacon.

Okay, I see what's going on here.

She doesn't want me to sleep with Brin's friend. She never thought I'd make it this far, and she's getting panicky. Can't bear it. Didn't think I could do it and wants to back out on our deal but she can't back out so this is what she resorts to. I know what this is. I read about it in Randy's word-a-day calendar. This is subterfuge.

I'll bet they're working together. They're in cahoots. Martin said he had that dream the other night that Brin was drizzling chocolate syrup into his mouth . . . I bet that wasn't even a dream!

Drop my napkin on the plate, push back from the table. "I'm not too hungry today."

Look at her face fall. That's right, babe. The only thing that'll make me want to sleep with this chick is the fact that you want it to happen even less than I do.

"I'll just eat some carrots."

Oh, I'm killing her. It's killing her!

Finally! This is actually kind of fun.

To: BrinM@compumail.net
From: Chercher@worknet.com
Subject: Brainstorming

Okay, we've gotten ourselves into something here.
   Brainstorming:

   • We each disguise ourselves as the woman in the picture
and have sex with our own husbands and they're none the
wiser. We use those intricate latex masks people wear to
disguise themselves as one another in those Tom Cruise
movies. This is the most practical option possible. The only
possible drawback: our faces disguised, our husbands
might still recognize us naked. I've got that birthmark,
Dierdre's got her happy trail.

   • We each disguise ourselves as the woman in the picture
using those elaborate Tom Cruise–type latex masks and
have sex with one another's husbands and they're none
the wiser. Just as practical as the last option, but gives us
fun, new novelty. The only possible drawback is that none
of us wants to sleep with one another's husbands.

   • Our husbands arrive at the hotel room to find their wife
there waiting for an evening of sensual adventure and hi-
jinks. "Surprise!" The advantage of this idea is that it's how
a Lifetime cable movie about our story would end. (I got
dibs on Valerie Bertinelli to play me; no fair saddling me
with Jo from *Facts of Life*!) The only drawback is that, while
I can't speak for Martin or Randy, my husband would di-
vorce me with a viciousness fueled by weeks and weeks of
low-carb lunches.

• We drug our husbands, they wake up, and we convince them this has all just been a dream. The only disadvantage is that no one but Randy would believe us.

• We drug our husbands, they wake up, and we convince them that they have slept with the happy hooker and all had a slam-bang good time. The only disadvantage to this is that, if they did go through with it, at least one of them would have pulled a muscle and they know it. Lacking that evidence, they won't believe us.

• We hire a prostitute.

Thoughts?

—C.

To: Chercher@worknet.com
From: BrinM@compumail.net
Subject: RE: Brainstorming

It's sort of been a while since Martin and I have even talked about the whole thing. I guess it's too much to hope for that the guys have sort of forgotten about the whole sex promise and are enjoying their healthier lifestyle as its own reward?

—Brin

MARTIN 265 POUNDS

"You see, Doctor Javers, my wife and I have this kind of special anniversary coming up and we want things to be really special and, well, a couple of times recently things didn't work exactly the way they're supposed to. I know that's normal, I just want it to be, well, less normal. . . ."

RANDY 254 POUNDS

". . . no, Dr. DePaulo, I'm not on any other medications, apart from this stuff for my attention span. No. And I'm not sure if I'm going to even need this, it's just that, well, I've seen all the ads and it sounds like something it would be good to have around because, you know, most of the time everything's great and my wife and I are nuts about each other so everything works fine, it's just that . . ."

DOUG 260 POUNDS

". . . the way I figure it, Dr. Newbaker, if science can
guarantee me a rock-solid boner, count me in."

To: BrinM@compumail.net
From: Chercher@worknet.com
Subject: RE: RE: Brainstorming

>>I guess it's too much to hope for that the guys have sort of forgotten about the
>>whole sex promise and are enjoying their healthier lifestyle as its own reward?

It's too much to hope for.

—C.

MARTIN 263 POUNDS

I'm not sure why, but I waited in the living room until Brin got home. A half dozen times I imagined hearing the car in the driveway even though you can't hear any car in the driveway from the living room. If a car plowed through the garage door, you probably wouldn't hear it from the living room. We've got that kind of house. The kind where you can't hear a car crashing into the garage from the living room.

So while sitting in the living room I realized that I haven't sat like that without music or TV or a book or someone talking in a long time. Not since Regan used to fall asleep on me while we watched something about monkeys on Animal Planet and I'd turn off the TV and let her lie there for a half an hour before I moved her to her bed. I miss those nights—nights when Philip would be at a sleepover—he was always at a sleepover—and the house would feel so empty. In a nice way.

Waiting for Brin in the quiet house felt . . . not good, exactly. Peaceful? Can something be peaceful but not necessarily good? Not that it was bad—it's just that it wasn't good or bad. It wasn't like that.

The point, though, is that I was waiting for Brin and when Brin finally walked through the door she looked at me like I was crazy because I was waiting there and I could tell that she thought I was waiting for her so that I could tell her some kind of terrible news. Like I was leaving.

Because I'm capable of that. I think I am. I don't have a reason and it's not something I want to do, but I think I could do it if I wanted to. If I had a reason. Which I don't.

"What?" she asked.

"Nothing at all," I said and walked over to her and started slow dancing with her.

"What's wrong with you?" she said, slowly starting to move her body to the imaginary music that I was hearing.

I danced her out of her coat and we slowly spun toward the stereo. When I turned the radio on, though, music erupted that didn't at all fit our moves.

"Off," she said at the same time that I was shutting it off.

"Are you trying to seduce me," she whispered in my ear.

"Honestly, no," I said. "I've just been thinking all day about dancing with you."

So we danced for, I don't know, a half hour? Forty-five minutes? Whatever it was.

And for the first time in—Weeks? Months? Maybe a couple of years?—I felt married. Like our vows meant something.

Dear Mr. De Niro,

A while back, I wrote you a letter—not exactly a fan letter but I suppose since I'm a fan of yours and it was, in fact, a letter, then it was kind of a fan letter. But from a regular person, not someone who is going to stalk you or anything. I haven't even seen all of your films, although you might recall that in the previous letter I mentioned Stanley and Iris, *which I know isn't one of your better-known flicks. (I hope you aren't one of those guys who insists on calling them "films" or "cinema" and gets bugged when someone says "movies" or "flicks." Did you ever do one of those "Inside the Actors Studio" things? What is that guy's name? The host? I hate that guy.)*

Anyway, the point of my last letter was to ask your advice on losing weight, since you so impressively lost so much that you had gained for Raging Bull *and you seem very healthy. I'm writing you now to tell you not to worry about it. Things are working great and I'm losing weight pretty consistently.*

See, my wife and her friends came up with this motivational thing that I'd love to tell you about because it would make a great movie or book (did you ever write a book? I'm not sure). If you are interested, I really would like to talk to you about it and would even fly out to LA or New York if I knew that we had a meeting for that purpose. Of course, I would expect you to take a percentage of whatever happens with the project. You could do very well with this and it might keep you from having to make another comedy so that you could do another Scorsese movie or something instead of a lot of the stuff you've done recently, which I'm sure you just did for money (I'm not knocking that, of course. Hell, I never turned down a paycheck, right?).

Even if you're not interested in that, I just wanted to let you know not to worry about the weight thing.

Randy Tonelli

To: BrinM@compumail.net
From: Chercher@worknet.com
Subject: RE: Quick Semiemergency Question

I spent from noon to two today trolling the Internet googling such combos as "massage parlors" and "Chicago," "hookers" and "Indiana," and "prostitutes" and "Midwest." I've got, I think, some good information and will try to make some calls (from a pay phone) tomorrow.

Right now, though, I've got a problem. . . . HOW DO YOU MAKE POP-UPS STOP!!!!!!

MARTIN 263 POUNDS

We went on a real live date. Brin and I. Went to the touring Broadway musical that came through town. We go to those sometimes, or used to; Brin has a handle on which ones are supposed to be good, she likes to see them. This one was all marionettes and puppets and big headwear with faces, though, and I gotta say—when did grown-ups start paying top dollar for puppet shows?

I didn't even care, though, and here's why: It's been awhile since we've been to one of these touring shows, which means it's been awhile since I've been in that auditorium, and the thing is? I fit. In the seats. Really well or, anyway, better than I used to. It was almost comfortable. And that was so satisfying that I found myself for the first time in history wishing a play had been longer.

The date was nice for other reasons, too, of course, a good time overall. But that seat, fitting in that seat—! I'm wondering where one buys one of those theater seats. I didn't even mind Brin insisting on buying the CD that she'll never listen to.

DOUG 253 POUNDS

Here's how it's supposed to be. You're fat. You don't get laid. You are looked down on at work.

I don't want to get into what's happening in my sex life.

It's what's happening in my business life that's really pissing me off. Specifically, I get called into Joe Phillips's office today and he's staring down at his desk and he's got something up on his computer that I can't see and he says that I have to stop forwarding jokes to people because some of them are offensive and that, off the record, that didn't bother him so much but now that my productivity is down and my sales are off and my blah blah bullshit, he's been told by human resources to review my file and he hates to do that and wants to be up front with me.

And I know what's going on. They don't like to fire people based on performance because that implies that we're not performing as a company. And they don't like to fire fat people because then they get accused of firing fat people. They like to find some other reason so that we disappear quietly and don't say a word and forwarding dirty jokes is a good way to do it.

Thing is, I'm careful about that shit. I never forward anything naked and I never forward anything where there's an ethnic thing in it, even if it's funny. I don't even forward the dumb blond jokes. Still, in this fucking world anything you do is going to offend someone, and I don't want to ask him what he's got on me.

"What's the answer?" I ask him. "Describe a scenario where I'm still working here a year from now."

I didn't like how long he waited.

"I can't see the future," he says. "But I suppose if your numbers, I don't know, double or something, then it would be very difficult to see you leave."

They liked the fat guy.

They don't seem to think much of this new guy.

I've got a good mind to screw Joe's wife.

MARTIN 262 POUNDS

Another pound.

Jesus, if I don't win this . . . If I don't reach the goal, how does that look? Brin came up with the idea. It's Brin's friend. If Doug and Randy get a one-way ticket to hooker-land and I don't, then I can't see how our little three sets of friends gatherings can continue. Did Brin and Cheryl and Dierdre think this through? Do they know what hell they will be bringing down on me if I don't make it?

RANDY 249 POUNDS

Exactly what they tell you exactly pain in the arm intense pain in the arm I've had other ones before and I thought, "I'm having a heart attack" but this is different this is I'M HAVING A HEART ATTACK MOTHER OF GOD I DON'T WANT TO DIE MY CHEST IS EXPLODING PLEASE LET ME DIE PLEASE LET ME DIE I DON'T WANT TO DIE PLEASE LET ME DIE Hail Mary full of grace the lord is with thee I somehow pull over to the side of the road and somehow get my seatbelt off and somehow open the door and somehow stumble around the car (the front way, I think, although it could have been around the back I don't know I don't know I don't know) and get to the curb and, I think, sit there and, I think, lie on my back and the brownish grass of the curb is under me along with something like a rock but not a rock and I didn't space it right because if I spaced it right my head would be on the softest part of the grass and even though MY CHEST IS EXPLODING I'd at least have that Hail Mary full of grace but instead, my head is on the concrete and I'm trying to find a tunnel through the pain to remember if I had pulled over on a populated street or on a quiet one which would make a big difference as to whether or not someone finds me and calls an ambulance or whether I just die here and I think I hear someone pulling over and I'm trying to get my cell phone out of my pocket but I think it's still in the car and so is my wallet because I take it out because I don't like riding with it while it indents my ass because somewhere I thought I read that a wallet in your back pocket while you sit causes your back to go out of whack and I don't want my back to go out of whack and I don't want this PAIN IN MY CHEST I don't want it I don't want it but it won't leave it's like your brother-in-law sleeping on your couch for the twelfth straight day it's got to stop it's got to stop this sledgehammer connected to the center of my rib cage and I don't know why Hail Mary keeps popping into my head instead of The Lord's Prayer or something else I think I only know two prayers there's got to be another one "Look out, I know CPR" I hear someone say and, even with MY CHEST EXPLOD-ING I'm thinking, "You ass, this guy"—me—"doesn't need CPR." I'm breathing. CPR is for when you stop breathing. I'm breathing. I've just got the thing from *Alien* bursting through my newly kind-of svelte frontage and I think my eyes are open and I think the guy's not going to do CPR on me and I think I'm sweating and sweating and sweating or something and I may have pissed myself and I may be dying and that guy saying he was going to do CPR may be the last voice I hear, which would be wrong, so stinking wrong because my life has to add up to more than that. It has to be Dierdre or Ty. Dierdre and Ty. Both. Together. A list in no particular order 1. Dierdre 2. Ty 3. This really kinda hurts seriously 4. God 5. my mom. And I hear their voices although I know they aren't there and I know that they are the center of my life and they are my strength and they are the reason I've done anything I've done and Dierdre is the one who I'll be with to the end of my days whether that's tomorrow or fifty years from now but in front of me, looking down on me, isn't Dierdre, it's the hooker college buddy and she's telling me to stay alive she's telling me to hold on she's telling me that I can take her slowly and build and build and build and build and this can't be good for my EXPLODING CHEST but it's got to be good for something because I feel myself rise off the ground like I'm David Copperfield's assistant who I think is really twins because I heard once that all magicians' assistants are twins, which explains a lot, and now 1. I'm done moving up and 2. I'm moving across and 3. It's darker and 4. I'm strapped down and 5. Something is over my mouth and 6. I hear a siren and there's got to be another prayer I might get through this I need to know her name I have to thank her and I do not love her I love Dierdre and those guys in the Bible didn't love the angels who visited them even though they were certainly more exciting than their wives they loved their wives maybe in a different way than we love our wives now because they were like goat herders and didn't have anything resembling indoor plumbing and they were told that women didn't do much thinking let alone have rights or anything and maybe they didn't ask permission of their wives when it came time to do some humping and bumping when the guy wanted it he just did it whether she wanted it or not and those guys had lots of wives and the Bible thumpers point to places in the books where it says you can't be gay or you can't spill your seed but they don't point to the places where you can marry a bunch of people and where you can't eat pepperoni, which makes me hate those Bible thumpers, and MY CHEST IS STILL EX-PLODING and I think they loved their wives different from the angels but that didn't keep them from looking for the angels and hoping for the angels and wishing for the angels and she is back and she's lying next to me as if we've just finished the deed and she wants me to rest and she's staring at the ceiling with a smile on her face because even though she's a whore, I want her to be a satisfied whore, which would make the whole thing better for me, which, I guess, means that I'm being selfish in wanting to please her but she doesn't seem to mind any of that she just knows that in the stillness of her body she is getting me through the worst like when I was trying to talk Dierdre through the contractions that brought Ty closer and closer to personhood and DAMN IT HURTS IT HURTS IT HURTS IT HURTS and if Ty being pushed out of Dierdre hurt this much how the hell do women have more than one kid maybe I'm crying like a baby or maybe my face is frozen in some kind of crazed grimace but she's there with her head on my chest and her hair has something that softens the pain just a little just enough just a little to get me through get me through get me through and the Grimace used to be one of the McDonaldland characters but you don't see so much of him anymore or the Hamburglcr which somebody probably said is a bad role model as if we look to hamburger chain characters as role models or maybe they did a study that determined that theft of food at McDonald's was higher when the Hamburglar was part of the team and wouldn't that then mean that all those animated thieves in cereal commercials (the Trix rabbit, Fred and Barney Rubble and all those guys) are leading to thefts of the cereal and DAMN DAMN DAMN DAMN I'm dying and I'm thinking of her and not my wife and I'm thinking about the Hamburglar and the Trix rabbit and not life and truth and God and love and something is in me and something is fighting it and something is trying to make me sleep and something is trying to make me die and die and die and die and die and die and die and though Dierdre will still be here on Earth the whore who I have never met will come with me wherever I go she's with me because she doesn't yet have a body and I have to give her a body by seeing her and she's here in me with me now and she whispers in my ear without moving my body that I have to live because I have to, for one night, know her and make her real and I always thought that that was an awkward phrase "know her" like it came from the glossary of prudity but here it makes sense it makes sense through the pain and through MY EXPLODING CHEST that I have to touch her if I do nothing else if I lie there and don't do a thing if Mr. Johnson stages a sit-down strike and if she says, "go on, it's paid for" but nothing happens because of my love for Dierdre or my nerves or doctor's orders because of this HEART ATTACK I'm having then I still need to need to need to need to walk into the room and shut the door and touch her connect with her my flesh to her

lou harry and eric pfeffinger

214

flesh whether it's me buried deep inside her or if it's my hand touching her face I need to make her real to change her from an idea in my head to a person of flesh and blood who lives and will die and I don't want to die and she doesn't want me to die and I touch her need to touch her need to live for that live for that live for that.

MARTIN 255 POUNDS

Jesus, Randy. What the hell did you do to yourself?

RANDY 247 POUNDS

It happened.

I had a heart attack.

I thought that was a possibility. I did. Grandpop had three of them, why shouldn't I get one?

But I always thought of it in the future or the present, never in the past.

Just the other day, I HAD a heart attack.

Done.

Done that.

Been there, done that.

Put a fork in it. It's done.

Everyone's looking at me as if I'm going to have some insight into life now. Like I'll have seen the error of my ways or something. Ty said to me, "Geez, that must've sucked."

He's right. It sucked. It hurt. Bad. Still does. Although these pain pills are mighty fine.

Here's what I said to Dierdre: "These things are supposed to change you. But I don't feel changed."

And then I told her: "We were good before. We're good now. And I know I'm supposed to do some serious soul-searching now and find the error of my ways, but the fact is, you already did that. You found the error of my ways. The error of my ways was that I didn't get the fact that in order to spend more days with you, I needed to take care of myself. I ate like Arnold Ziffel at an Old Country Buffet. Can't blame that on glands. Can't blame that on anyone or anything. You figured out how to get me to lose it. You saved my life."

And then she cried and said that the heart attack was her fault and I told her that if I hadn't lost the weight, the heart attack might have killed me and then we hugged and cried and I started to get my first postcardiological-collapse woody and all felt right with the world.

DOUG 249 POUNDS

Martin didn't call me until about eight and by that time they knew that Randy wasn't going to die or anything and so they kept me out of that really ugly everything-in-slow-motion time. I didn't have to bother reassessing my life or figuring out what I could do different or any of that mortality shit. Instead, it was one of those calls that started with, "Now listen, he's okay now, but . . ." so it's all, like, in flashback for me. You know in movies when someone's telling the story and there's a flashback and that person is in danger and you shouldn't be scared for them or anything because you know that they survive. *Saving Private Ryan* kind of pissed me off that way. You think it's a flashback from one guy and then it turns out to be a flashback by another guy. Bait and switch.

My point, though, is that it was like I got the scene where Randy's okay and in the hospital first before I got the scene where he's lying on the side of the road grabbing at his chest so I missed a ride on the "Is he gonna die or isn't he" roller coaster that Martin and Brin and Dierdre and Cheryl rode. I mean, why should they blame me for not getting all weepy? They can't blame me if they talk and talk about how intense and scary the roller-coaster ride was and I can't really relate because I was over somewhere buying cotton candy. I'm sure as hell glad he's alive, isn't that enough?

That should be the basis of a religion. Not all the other bullshit, just being glad that someone else is alivc. Sure as hell would cut down on the time you have to spend in church.

Maybe Randy will be sick enough that we can skip Cheryl's nephew's wedding this Saturday. If I've got to go to another fringe relative's birthday and fucking line dance, I'm going to climb a bell tower and start shooting.

They still have bell towers, yeah?

RANDY 241 POUNDS

Here's the sick thing. I haven't seen my mother in, what, six years. Never came up from Florida since she went down. Never wanted to talk to me since she and Dad split up. Thought I sided with him.

But she makes the trek up because her only son is in the hospital and I don't even know she's coming. Dierdre tells me that Mom's on the way up and for a minute I don't know who she means by Mom and then it occurs to me that this means my mother and I try to flash back to every fight and to a greatest hits listing of the stupid things she's said and done including:

1. Telling her children at various times who her favorite offspring is at any given point, as though that one's not going to run off and immediately tell the other ones.

2. Saying to the wife of one of her offspring, "Is that how you wanted your hair to look?"

3. Riding in the backseat and talking about her offspring's driving, saying things like "Don't do that, people carry guns in their cars now!" Her idea of defensive driving is not getting shot.

4. Planning a trip to Europe over Christmas break during my freshman year of college—without telling me or inviting me along. The upside of that incident is that I

was going to surprise her by bringing home Dierdre to meet her. End result: A holly, jolly Christmas and a wonderful tradition of ringing in the New Year (we've stayed home every year since).

So Mom walks into the hospital room and she's still dressed like it's Florida and she doesn't say, "How are you feeling?" and she doesn't say "Thank God you're alive" and she doesn't say "Just tell me what I can do."

Instead, she takes one look at me and says, "You look good. Have you lost weight?"

To: BrinM@compumail.net
From: Chercher@worknet.com
RE: RE: RE:

I could've sworn I told you about this thing. It's no big deal actually, except in my twisted self-absorbed mind.

You're going to make me tell you, right? I know you, you with your probing questions and your pathological fascination with all things Cheryl. Just as well . . . probably rather tell you like this than say it all out loud anyway. Especially since I thought I'd already told you out loud once anyway. What's that about? Who did I tell out loud?

I'd been out of school like a year. This was the period when Doug and I were broken up, since after graduation I'd determined in my youthful foolishness that I deserved more from life than Doug. What I lacked in money and friends I made up for with loneliness and self-doubt. Never mind that college had been hard on me anyway, you know about that.

So, tired old story, same old same old: I'm at a bar, not a big bustling bar where people cycle in and out in great waves and meet other people but a little almost like neighborhood kind of bar where I swear I was the only one there who didn't know anybody. Then as now, my judgment and instincts were impeccable.

Sitting, drinking alone in silence, and about five minutes before last call this guy I'd noticed strikes up a conversation with me, he approaches me. I had noticed him, too: He wasn't "cute" in a "cute" way, but cute in this way that I've always had a secret shameful weakness for. Skinny but fit, pale, smart-looking, with glasses, a nerdy-but-confident thing, like he's comfortable about his superiority to all the better-looking guys. Other girls want Superman, I've always fantasized about Clark Kent, go figure. I love the guys who file remote reports from the field in newscasts but are never going to be in the anchor chair.

"But Cheryl, then, why Doug?" Yeah. I want Clark Kent, why do I marry Captain Caveman? That's a story for another day.

Anyway, we're conversing, it's almost comfortable, nearly enjoyable, last call comes, we're back at my place making the two-backed beast, it's all terribly romantic. But if you could imagine how improbably psyched I was about it. I was actually like "Thank God if I'm going to have impetuous ill-advised sex with a stranger, thank God at least he isn't too good-looking." Like this made me less shallow, see.

What does this have to do with anything? Well, Clark Kent didn't stay the night. That's fine. He had to go after some minimal after-the-fact dozing. Okay, fine. He left a stack of cash on the bookshelf as he left. Yeah, that's what destroyed me.

So if I'm weirding out, that's probably why. And come to think of it maybe now we know why I married Doug instead of a Clark Kent.

Delete message. Wipe hard drive. Erase your own memory. Burn it down and salt the earth.

xxxooo

>>BrinM@compumail.net wrote:
>>What thing? When? You never told me. Spill.
>>>>You wrote:

  >>>>Sorry if I've been acting so weirded out, B. Whole
business is getting to me a little bit, probably because of that
thing after college I told you about.

To: Randy12479@aol.com
From: Doug@linklink.com

Hey Martin. Get this.

I'm visiting Randy yesterday afternoon between appointments and when I get there he's in the middle of watching a *Murder She Wrote*. What the fuck is the deal with that? I know he had his heart attack and he can't do much, but jeez. It would be one thing if he was sleeping and it happened to be on. But I could tell that he was half listening to me and half listening to the show so he could find out who the fuck did the murder or stole the old lady's knitting needles or whatever the hell it is they did on that show. Is there anything stupider than these mysteries where some small town faces crime after crime after crime and some little old pain-in-the-ass lady solves all the crimes? Why would Randy watch—let alone like—this shit? Should we be worried?

—Doug

Doug E. Garrison, Sales Manager
T.H.E. Solutions, "Better people through business"
One Park Plaza

The only thing you should be worried about is figuring out how to work your e-mail. You sent that note to me, not Martin.

But since you raised the point, I'll say this:

First, go to hell.

Second, I wasn't trying to hear who committed the crime since I had already seen that episode when it was originally aired.

Third, I'll take this opportunity to come out of the closet— yes, I do enjoy *Murder She Wrote*. I also liked *Barnaby Jones* back in the day. And before you sneer, consider this: These shows aren't that much different from the comic books that you read (yes, I know about your comic book collection— and the fact that you buy one to save and one to read). Do you really believe that Batman caught the Joker, what, three hundred times over the past whatever years and they can't keep him in jail? Do you really think that that much fighting can go on in the skies over a major metropolis without . . . to hell with it. I'm not going to argue with you. Just know that I'm sick of your condescending crap.

—Randy

"Win one for the Gipper."

To: MBB@yahoo.com
From: Doug@linklink.com

Hey Martin, read the attached exchange.

  Do you think Randy is really pissed at me? I can't tell from the e-mail and I'm kind of afraid to call him. This could be the first long-term friendship ended because of Angela Lansbury.

—Doug

Doug E. Garrison, Sales Manager
T.H.E. Solutions, "Better people through business"
One Park Plaza

CHERRY6: Hey.

INQUISITIVE_BRIN: Hey.

CHERRY6: Newbie?

INQUISITIVE_BRIN: I don't know what that means.

CHERRY6: That's a yes.

CHERRY6: Still there?

INQUISITIVE_BRIN: I'm just figuring out what I'm doing here. I'm new. Oh, newbie, I get it.

CHERRY6: What do you look like?

INQUISITIVE_BRIN: Oh, just normal, I guess. Mostly I have questions.

CHERRY6: This is a place to explore and experiment. Why don't you touch yourself and tell me how it feels.

INQUISITIVE_BRIN: No thank you. Is everyone here really midwesterners? From the Midwest?

INQUISITIVE_BRIN: Or are you all pretending to be midwesterners? Is it a fetish? People turned on by politeness? And flat nasal accents?

CHERRY6: Mostly midwesterners.

INQUISITIVE_BRIN: Well, because I'm actually sort of looking for someone I could maybe meet with in real life.

CHERRY6: Whoa, zero to sixty!

CHERRY6: Meeting irl isn't everyone's bag. Not at first.

INQUISITIVE_BRIN: irl?

INQUISITIVE_BRIN: Oh I get it. In real life. Cool. That's like RMA—you know, "Remember Me Always"—in a high school yearbook.

INQUISITIVE_BRIN: I thought if people here were "bi" and sexually adventurous maybe I'd find someone willing to sleep with my husband and two other guys for money.

INQUISITIVE_BRIN: Hello?

INQUISITIVE_BRIN: Did I make a faux pas?

CHERRY6: What are you, a cop?

INQUISITIVE_BRIN: No.

INQUISITIVE_BRIN: Would you

INQUISITIVE_BRIN: Would you like me to be a cop?

CHERRY6: No.

CHERRY6: I might be interested in something like that.

CHERRY6: The thing with your husband.

CHERRY6: In exchange for something.

INQUISITIVE_BRIN: Yeah, I said. Money.

CHERRY6: Something else.

INQUISITIVE_BRIN: What esle/?

INQUISITIVE_BRIN: My typing gets

INQUISITIVE_BRIN: when I get flustered. What else?

CHERRY6: Describe yourself.

CHERRY6: Tell me.

INQUISITIVE_BRIN: I have a B.A. I read a lot. I'm not as confrontational as I'd like to be. Sort of scattered lately, my husband's friend is in the hospital. I think I multitask too much, take on too much.

CHERRY6: I meant physically.

INQUISITIVE_BRIN: I've got good verbal skills. Not as good with spatial

INQUISITIVE_BRIN: Oh. Sorry.

INQUISITIVE_BRIN: I'm 5'6".

CHERRY6: Touch yourself.

CHERRY6: Are you touching yourself?

INQUISITIVE_BRIN: Okay.

CHERRY6: How's it feel?

INQUISITIVE_BRIN: Okay.

CHERRY6: Mm, tell me.

INQUISITIVE_BRIN: It's not that great actually. I'm sort of uptight about keeping my keyboard clean.

CHERRY6: Are you as turned on as I am right now?

INQUISITIVE_BRIN: Probably less.

INQUISITIVE_BRIN: I thnki I'm porobbaly going to logo ff now.

CHERRY6: Uh huh, I bet. Going to touch yourself some more aren't you?

INQUISITIVE_BRIN: Sure.

INQUISITIVE_BRIN: Why not.

INQUISITIVE_BRIN: Oh my God wait.

INQUISITIVE_BRIN: You're a guy, aren'y you!?/

CHERRY6: FUCK HOW COULD YOU TELL YOU FUCKING BITCH???????????

>>>>SESSION TERMINATED.

RANDY 240 POUNDS

"My father used to be so fat," says Ty.

"How fat was he?" I ask. And then he goes on. Every time he comes to the hospital he has ten more lines and most of them are actually pretty funny. Only I'm not supposed to laugh too hard. So I give each one a score. Ty keeps track of the average.

"So fat that when he wore brown he looked like a UPS truck."

"So fat that when we went to the beach people kept trying to roll him back into the ocean."

"So fat that he got in trouble for affecting the tides."

Like I said, some are better than others. The last day I'm here, though, no matter how good the fat dad jokes are, I'm going to give him all perfect tens.

DOUG 247 POUNDS

Wow, so it's been a year. A whole year of dieting and exercise, of having this mysterious prostitute hanging over my head and of even more marital weirdness than usual. This bullshit has taken a year of my life. What if it takes two years? What if it takes three? At what point are the years allegedly added to my life made negligible by the number of fucking miserable years I spent adding them?

No one else seems to have noticed the milestone, between Randy's thing and everything else. I deserve a reward. I'm going to have a Filet-O'fucking-Fish.

Then maybe log on to that bisexual midwesterner site, chat with some of the ladies.

MARTIN 247 POUNDS

Once she got the news, Amy insisted on meeting me at the hospital and, after commenting again on my semi-svelte self ("Wow, Martin," she said, "you look younger than you looked when you were younger"), she insisted on going up to see Randy. She always liked Randy. I think she always liked Randy. Never liked Doug. Always was a pretty good judge of character. Or the lack thereof.

Why do I keep hoping that she's going to tell me that she and Perfect Guy have split? Again. The best I could piece together was that they split the first time about six months after she moved to Ohio. Then got back together about a year later. Who the hell knows. I just know she's back with him now and what I want to have happened is that she caught him ordering used tampons from a fetish site or he was nabbed embezzling from an organization that raises funds for orphaned cripples.

I have no idea what I would do if she gave me that information, but every freaking time I see her I'm hoping that that's the info she's delivering. I really, really want to have that soul-searching "What do we do now" conversation. Half the time I think about it, the scene ends with me telling her that she blew it. That she had her chance. That Brin has been there for me. The other half of the time, I can't recall Brin's face.

Really, really strange to wake up and see Martin and Amy standing over the bed. For a second there . . . no, not really a second, less than that, I didn't have any clue where I was. It's been a long time since Amy was in the picture—since she was an integral part of us.

"Hey, buddy," she said, and took my hand. Took it. Not an offer but a taking. Like nothing was different. Nothing was wrong. My exploding chest set the world back a couple of years.

I smiled. I talked to her about Ty and about her kids. I talked to her about the weight-loss thing and how, yeah, it was cool that us guys were doing this together and that we should be on *Oprah* or something. I complained about the hospital food and asked her how Ohio was treating her.

And all the while I tried not to look at Martin because Martin, well, I don't know what's going on with Martin. I haven't really known what's going on with Martin in a long time. I had my heart explode. He had his heart ripped out.

There was an uncomfortable few seconds of silence

and Martin excused himself to use the restroom. After the door shut, something just snapped in me. Not snapped, really. It was like a wall dropped. Resistance was gone. An obstacle out of the way. And then I said, very quietly, "Listen. It was very nice of you to come by here. And I know we haven't seen each other in years. . . ."

She smiled.

". . . But I have to tell you . . . and I can tell you because I'm a guy who just had a heart attack . . . that it's very difficult to lie here and have a pleasant conversation with you because you left my friend Martin and took away his kids who he loves more than anything and . . ." I took a slow, steady breath, like the doc told me. ". . . I just don't want to look at you. I don't want to look at someone who could do that, could tear apart not only your family but a group of friends, who could do that and think that it's okay. I thought we were going to watch our kids grow up together. I thought that was part of the plan."

She seemed torn between trying to hug me and doing an "I don't have to stand for this."

"Randy, I didn't come here for . . ."

"Of course you didn't. Who would? But there's all of Ohio for denial."

"You don't know everything about . . ."

"About what? Did he cheat on you?"

"He might have."

"He didn't."

"He took a condom with him on a business trip."

"Did he come back with it?"

"Well . . ."

"Then he didn't cheat on you."

"He could've bought a new one, maybe."

"Did he hit you? No."

"Set the bar a little lower, why don't you, Randy."

"Did he bust his ass to take care of the kids? Yes. Did he love you with everything he had?"

Nothing. Nothing at all.

"Martin got fat. That's what it was. You didn't want to be married to a fat guy."

Very quietly, she said, "I don't know."

"Well," I said. "Not knowing isn't a damn good reason for ending a marriage."

"It's nice to see him the way he used to be."

When I stopped to take another slow breath, she just said, "You take care of yourself" and went for the door.

"Wait," I said, a little too dramatically, knowing I was already in a place where I had no business being. "I'm saying this because I've got a strong feeling he's still nuts about you. He loves Brin, but he's nuts about you. And you may not be thinking about it now but there is likely to be a time when you think about him again. You've cheated on one husband. No reason to think you wouldn't cheat on another.

"But the thing is," I go on, "you can't do anything about it. You let something like that happen and you'll wreck his life again. You'll screw with the kids' minds. And you'll be hurting Brin, and Brin's good people."

"I'm not interested in Martin."

"You heard what I said."

"I'm not."

And she left. And I wasn't sure if I had helped prevent a disaster or put a very bad idea in her head.

MARTIN 246 POUNDS

Amy was already in the hall when I came back from the restroom. I peeked in and told Randy I'd see him tomorrow. Then I walked her down to the waiting room, where the kids were hanging out.

She told them to behave and to listen to their father.

She hugged them—a part that always kills me—and told me to make sure they called her every day. If things had been different, we might have had a long talk about what happened to Randy and how they didn't have to worry because he would be fine. But the kids hardly know Randy anymore and they didn't have questions so instead we went to the playground and they spent most of the time on the merry-go-roundish thing that spins around. Philip and Regan kept saying "faster, faster" so instead of just standing there, grabbing each bar as it came by and whipping it past me, I took hold of one bar and ran it around and around and around.

DIERDRE

For my final speech I'd like to start by thanking Mr. Nelson for teaching such a great public-speaking class; I think we've all learned a lot here. Because they say that people's number one fear in the world is speaking in front of a group of people, which, when you think about it, is probably a pretty good sign that most people don't have enough to be afraid of. Because I've been through some things lately that make me think there are much more important things to be afraid of, if you think about it. I'd rather speak in front of a group of people than have my husband die of a heart attack, for example. I'd rather speak in front of a group of people than be alone. I'd rather speak in front of a group of people than raise my son as a single mother. I'd rather speak in front of a group of people than be the widow at a funeral and that's not even because I don't have any black clothes.

I'd also rather speak in front of a group of people than be buried in snakes, but that's probably neither here or there.

Basically, there are much scarier things than speaking in front of this group of people, especially since you're all so nice and supportive. If you were a group of people with tazers—you know, those things that the police use when a guy is too drunk to understand "stop or I'll shoot" but they don't want to shoot him—if you were a group of people like that, I might actually be as afraid as I'm supposed to because, well, you could hurt me. With the tazers. But since you don't have tazers or any other weapons, I'm not afraid of speaking in front of any of you. I used to be afraid of you, Jimmy, because of the way your eyes point in different directions, but I'm totally past that now.

I'm not even afraid of the fact that Mr. Nelson's going to give me a bad grade on this speech because it's a speech about global warming, or was supposed to be, but I don't know where I stand on global warming because I don't know a lot about it—I know I like wearing sweaters, so that's con, but it also, I guess, raises the level of the ocean, and who doesn't like the ocean, so there's that. But what I know a lot about is your husband having a heart attack, which just goes to show there are some things you'd rather not know a lot about.

Thank you, the end.

RANDY 228 POUNDS

For Halloween Dierdre told Ty he could use one of my old belts as his Indiana Jones bullwhip, if it's not too long.

Halloween is awesome.

To: BrinM@compumail.net
From: Chercher@worknet.com
Subject: Pretty women

B—

So Randy's out of the woods. That's good. Now we can focus on the way we've helped to make our lives completely fall apart by embracing the lifestyle of deceit and sin. I talked to Dierdre this morning, just to check on Randy, and she said to take her mind off his heart attack (she's still rattled) she's been working on finding us a, um, you know, "candidate." For the "job." You know, of "fucking" our "husbands."

Euphemisms are overrated.

So because she's heard that a lot of these people work under the umbrella of being massage artists, she's been picking up the free weekly paper and calling those numbers in the ads in the back. She's gotten something like nine full-body massages from different women. She's considerably poorer than she used to be, but verrrrrrrrrrrrrrrrrrrrrrrrrrry relaxed.

But apparently none of these women is a secret prostitute. At least, that's what Dierdre gathered from what she described as her subtle interrogation of them. Given Dierdre's talent for subtlety, I'm guessing this nuanced subterfuge took the form of asking them "So do you also have sex with men for money?"

What's our next step? Going to the street corner? What street corner? Every corner I can think of has a Starbucks or a Quizno's, not so much sex industry professionals.

Stymied,

C.

To: Chercher@worknet.com
From: BrinM@compumail.net
Subject: RE: Pretty women

C,

Halt your street corner plans. Just talked to Dierdre, and apparently masseuse number fourteen gave her some phone numbers. She claims these are professionals of the "high-class" variety, the ones who get on the news when they're arrested and are hired by the Baldwin brothers or Charlie Sheen.

—Brin

P.S. You know that book club I was always trying to drag you into? Well, I just quit. They wanted to impose a 319-page rule. Nothing over 357 pages could be suggested. What the hell is wrong with people?

DOUG 242 POUNDS

Is it wrong of me to hate Randy because while I'm doing abdominal crunches and leg lifts, he's lying in a bed because a doctor told him to?

Of course it's not. If the hatred drives me to keep exercising, it's a force for good. Randy would want it this way. If he were dead, which he's not. I'm sure he would tell me as much if I called him. Which I'm not going to do.

MARTIN 251 POUNDS

As I'm walking across the park with Randy, he brings it up and I'm glad he brings it up because I wasn't going to bring it up.

He says to me, "Here's what the doc told me—and this is in front of Dierdre. He says that we have to wait at least two weeks before having sex. And we kind of say, 'Okay. Fine' and Dierdre, who is sitting down and happens to have her purse open, quietly opens up her calendar book and acts like she's erasing something on one day and writing it into another and I'm like Harvey Korman trying to keep from cracking up in Tim Conway's face and then he says, he really says, 'And you can't have sex with anyone else for more than a month,' and Dierdre kind of bites her lip and I'm ready to lose it and I try to look like I don't know what he means because I'm suddenly not sure if he says this to everyone or if he's saying this to me."

"You were wondering if Dierdre told the doctor something," I said.

"Right," said Randy. "Then I was really uncomfortable and I guess the doc sensed that and said that he's got to tell this to all couples because if he just told it to some, people would think he was making judgments and he's not in the business of making judgments. It seems that guys who are having affairs are more stressed and therefore more susceptible to repeated heart episodes."

"How's it been," I ask him, "with Dierdre? I mean, before the heart thing." I'm hoping he knows what I mean because I don't want to ask any other way.

"Pretty good," he says. "I mean, we're always pretty good. Pretty happy in the morning. Pretty cool at dinner. Usually nice at night."

"Things have been different with Brin," I tell him. "A little."

"A little better or a little worse."

"A little more . . . verbal. We talk a lot more. In bed. She wants me to tell her stories. To make shit up."

"And this is good? Bad?"

"Different," I say. "I'm not a storyteller. I made up a couple of things when she started asking and that was fine but she didn't want to hear the same ones over and over again. I try to remember scenes from porno films I've seen—I haven't seen a lot of them but, you know. Didn't remember many real scenes there, though—not much more than the 'I'm here to fix the plumbing' or 'Who called for a pizza?'"

"You haven't seen much porn lately, have you?" he asked.

"Not really."

"You got two extremes now," said Randy. "You've got the ones with the high production values and you've got the pure amateur get-right-down-to-it thing."

"Is that what you do when Dierdre goes out?"

"No. We usually watch them together."

"You're shittin' me?"

"What can I tell you? She likes the girl-on-girl ones. I'm the luckiest man in the Midwest."

We just go around the park once. He wanted to get some air. And when I get him back to his house I'm trying to think of all the places where he could hide his stash of porno tapes. I imagine there's a stash. He sounded like he'd seen a lot and there aren't many video stores anymore that have the little back room. Blockbuster's got nothing worse than R, I don't think. And I can't picture him going to Phil's Diamond Video or The Gentlemen's Hut. Maybe he orders them through the Internet. Maybe there's some kind of Amway-like system where you become a customer, then you become a distributor and you make money from all the people you sign up who sign up other people, creating this gigantic porn pyramid with a nearly unlimited supply of guys willing to join up at the bottom. There might even be a blackmail component. Some pop-up that says that, since you visited some gang bang site or something, then the powers that be at the top of the pyramid will tell your mother unless you sign up as a distributor. Then there's a Porn Pyramid convention in Vegas and everyone wears badges.

We never really finished the conversation. I was going to tell him that when it comes to Brin wanting to hear stories I was out of ideas and that I had stolen just about every plot from Cinemax and *Red Shoe Diaries* that I could remember.

She got into the stories but at first didn't want to be a character in them. Later she seemed to like making appearances in the stories, first as walk-ons and then right in the heat of the action.

Maybe she'll want to join me and hooker friend. Maybe she thinks that if we talk about these sorts of kink fests enough, then her inviting herself into hooker night wouldn't seem so extreme. Not sure how I feel about that. On the one hand, I never managed to even come close to making a three-way happen. There was a moment in college when I was necking with a girl and another came into the room and I kind of invited her to join us but the first girl slapped my hand. That's about it.

But is this the three-way I'd want? If it happened the other way—if the deal was a three-way with Brin and a hooker—that would be one thing. But now it's her cutting in on my night with her friend. It's really a pretty weasely move, if you think about it.

If that's what she's doing.

And if it is, damn, maybe she had one of those "college experiences" with this girl. Maybe this is the only way she can have that thrill again and still believe she never had cheated on her husband. Of course, if that's the case and the two of them did go at it one drunken night junior year, then why should hooker girl charge her for the three-way? If your accountant friend does your taxes for free one year, he can't expect you to pay him the next year. You offer, of course, but he turns you down and you know he's going to turn you down. In that case, though he's doing something not particularly fun for you. The three-way should, in theory, be fun for all three particularly considering that she and Brin had done it all already in college and I'm, well, not exactly a Chippendale but I'm looking pretty good lately. Better, at least. I'm assuming that Brin hasn't shown her before-and-after pictures or anything. Unless, of course, they are planning the three-way and hooker friend said, "I don't know, do you have a picture?" and all Brin had was one where I was at maximum. But why should she want to see a picture if she's a hooker? Surely she's been with guys a lot dumpier than me. Even how I looked then.

Man, how did Brin stay with a guy who looked like that? Why did she ever do the things she did with me?

I'll never figure that out. At some point, that me will seem like a different guy. It'll be my fat time and we'll look at old photo albums and people who I won't meet for a few years will say, "That can't be you," and Brin will smile so proud of me but when they ask that I'll just imagine the hooker friend with her legs open and I'm not sure if that's what I want to picture. Or I'll picture Brin and her in the "He's done, let's keep going" two-way portion of the three-way and I don't think that's what I'm going to want to remember either. I worked my ass off and lost a shitload of weight. I want to remember how hard I worked to do this, to transform myself, to become something better, to live longer.

And Randy almost died doing it.

I was planning on going to the gym and running on the treadmill for a half hour but what I want to do right now is go home and take a nap.

I want to be rested for tonight. I'm going to tell Brin the story of the guy who catches his wife with a hooker on her birthday and, rather than get mad, joins in on the fun. We'll see how that one works.

Brin's Plan for Candidate Interviews

Preliminary remarks, introductions, niceties. Thanks for coming, we appreciate your time and your interest, can we get you anything to drink, that's a beautiful skirt, etc. Questions:

How long have you been doing this?

Do you have any references from ~~satisfied customers~~ past clients?

~~Do you have any~~ May we see your medical history?

What would you identify as your strengths and weaknesses ~~as a~~ in what you do?

Identify a time when you faced a significant challenge ~~as a~~ in what you do, and tell us briefly how you handled it.

If you weren't doing this, what would you like to do instead and why?

Is there anything you won't do for a client, or things that would kick us into a higher price structure, and to what degree does that need to be settled up front?

What strategies do you use to ~~stay limber~~ ~~flexible~~ ~~fit~~ keep up with the demands of your career? Do you have to do any professional reading? To stay apprised of new developments?

Do you have a policy in place to address the needs of dissatisfied clients?

lou harry and eric pfeffinger

Have you ever ever ever ever been in a situation quite like this before?

Closing remarks, good-byes, we hope to contact everyone with our decisions within the week, I can take your glass thanks, where did you get that skirt, etc. etc.

Cheryl's Interview Questions for the Common Slatterns

Can we see your medical history?

Do your parents know you're doing this? If so, what did they say? If not, what would they think?

When you were a little girl, what did you want to do when you grew up?

How long have you been doing this? Do you have any regrets? Do you ever wake up in the middle of the night cold and slick with sweat and self-loathing?

Is it ever fun?

Have you ever told a client after the fact "It's on the house"? And why?

What's your favorite thing about your job? Least favorite?

Have you ever been married? Do you have any colleagues in the business who went on to get married or have kids or lead a normal life? Did they leave the life behind? Or once it's in you will it never come out, do you think?

What was the first time like? Did you lie there thinking "I can't believe what's become of me"? Or were you thinking "This is supposed to be bad but it's not as bad as I thought it would be"?

What do you think as you sit there looking at us? What do you feel (about us)?

Have you ever read Gloria Steinem? Naomi Wolf? Andrea Dworkin? Jackie Collins?

Do you ever walk down the street or through a department store smiling at people and meeting people's gazes and thinking about how they have no idea what it is you do? Does it make you feel sexy, superior, inferior, or other?

Have you, seriously, have you ever done anything like this, with us and this thing we're doing? Are we, in your estimation, freaks, or are you currently judging us in any way?

Dierdre's Interview Questions for the person

1. We'll need to see your medical history.

2. How long have you been doing this?

3. How many guys, like, have you been with? How many girls?

4. I read somewhere that sometimes women in your profession spend so much time with men when they're on the clock that they prefer to be with women for their own fun. Any thoughts? [Explain "be with" if necessary]

5. Have you ever seen *Pretty Woman*? That's a pretty good movie. Does stuff in it make you mad like when doctors watch *Diagnosis Murder* or lawyers watch lawyer shows?

6. Take us through a typical date with a client. What do you do first? What do you do next? Do you have different plans you use depending on your professional instincts?

7. What's the dirtiest thing you've ever done for someone? The second-dirtiest? Third-dirtiest? [And so on.]

8. Do you think I could do what you do, or am I not, like, pretty enough? [Oh, thank you. No, you are, too.]

9. Would it be weird if I asked if I could feel your leg?

10. [Should one of us ask to kiss her, like a test-drive?]

11. I read about these things in the free weekly paper: "rimming," "catatasis," "water sports." Could you tell me what these things are?

12. Can you lift your leg over your head? [I can.]

13. Do you have a cheerleader uniform? [I do, still fits.]

14. [Should one of us ask to feel her hands?]

15. Do you ever videotape your sessions? And if so, are such videotapes available for perusal as part of this evaluation process?

16. Do clients ever ask you just to dance for them while they watch? And if so, what do you, then, do?

17. Do you ever get so hot and, like, erotic, just walking down the street or sitting in traffic, that you think your head is going to burst into flames?

18. Randy's really ticklish, I assume you have strategies for dealing with that?

19. Is this, what we're doing, the weirdest thing you've ever done? [If not, what is?]

RANDY 219 POUNDS

Here's another reason Doug should just shut up and doesn't know what he's talking about. Nobody should be that obsessed with Garrison Keillor, or whatever that guy's name is. Anyone who can go on and on about Garrison Keillor the way Doug can has no business talking crap about what somebody else might like or not like. I mean, I don't like that radio show either, heck, nobody does, I bet Mr. Keillor even in the middle of those little jaunty songs he sings stands there thinking "God this is awful." Thinking "I'm so ashamed." But nobody else talks about it. Better things to talk about. If you're going to go after *Prairie Home Companion,* might as well talk about some of the other lousy things you get on public radio, too; it's not like *Prairie Home Companion* is the only lousy thing on public radio. How about that other show, *Whad'ya Know?* or whatever it's called, even I can tell it's not smart enough to be on public radio. It's like a morning zoo program for public radio, only instead of two wisecracking hosts you have one and instead of a sound machine that makes farting noises he's got a jazz pianist. Not funny enough to be a morning zoo program, not smart enough to belong on public radio, why doesn't Doug talk about that once in a while? Guess its badness is too subtle for him. He misses out on, whatchacall, nuance. This is why he could never solve crimes like Jessica Fletcher.

Those guys who talk about fixing cars, too. I don't like them either. They know too much.

I don't listen to public radio much anyway. I like classic hits.

I turned off the TV to think because even when you're recuperating there's only so much TV you can take, but then I start thinking and look what I think about. No wonder people prefer TV. I'm going to turn it back on soon. The fact that *Murder She Wrote* is about to come on is pure coincidence.

Doug hasn't even called me, the jerko.

DOUG 235 POUNDS

You gotta look like the bad guy if you ignore somebody who had a heart attack so I gave a call to Randy even though he hasn't talked to me since the e-mail the other day and I asked him how he was doing and he said he was feeling better and there didn't seem much to talk about so I said maybe Martin and I could come over on Friday and shoot the shit and he said fine.

Damn, I feel like we're in high school and he's one of the girls I pissed off who would stay pissed off at me until my parents went out of town and I had another killer party and she would start to be nice to me again the Tuesday before the gig. At the party, she'd act like there was no problem and nothing ever happened.

I'm hoping Randy acts that way.

Because, to be honest, I don't have time for the bull-shit. I'm losing my job (probably). I'm losing my mojo (definitely). And that's plenty.

MARTIN 239 POUNDS

Doug wants me to go with him to see Randy this weekend. Total bullshit. This is like high school and, once again, I'm the guy trying to keep friends from fighting. Except in high school, they always made up by the weekend, when someone had a party. These two? Who the hell knows? Not to mention that meanwhile I'm fielding calls from Randy out of the blue, middle of the workday, Randy calling and asking if I thought it seemed like Doug's changed since he lost weight. Me going, "Changed how?" Randy saying, "I don't know, like he's less . . ." a pause while I know, I just know, he's flipping through that word-a-day calendar ". . . palatable. Less palatable?"

He mispronounces *palatable* but I know what he's talking about, even if I don't say so. I have a feeling Doug's exactly the same now as he was before he lost the weight but that it comes off differently now, like all that fat was cushiony insulation that muffled the effects of all the anger and surliness and misanthropy roiling deep inside. Now he's not so fat and that stuff's closer to the surface and it has unpleasant poky edges. Maybe fat guys aren't jolly after all; they're just well insulated.

But I don't share that with Randy. I don't share that because he seems to have forgotten that we don't discuss friendships, we just have them. Seriously, this isn't high school.

There's nothing like high school parties anymore. There's none of the danger of parents being away. None of the sense that there's anything at stake. We've got ten times the reason to get drunk or get high than we did in high school but one-tenth the motivation. Why is it so hard to get wasted at a grown-up party? How come there's never anybody to carry to the car? Okay, so a couple of beers watching a game can make us a little wobbly, but that's about it.

The other thing is, in high school you always ran into your friends. Out here you can say "I don't want to see Joe Blow" and, unless you worked with him, you wouldn't have to see him. Easy. Wanting to see someone is a choice. *Not* seeing someone is the default setting.

In high school, I liked the whole dating thing. College was pretty good, too. People were in your world. Meetings weren't accidental. In high school, someone told you that this girl liked you and you decided if you could talk yourself into liking her and then you started going out. Or she was there at a party and you were there at a party and the next thing you know, you're all over each other on a pile of coats in some dude's parents' bedroom. Bingo. You were dating—even if you never actually went on a date.

College was kind of the same thing, only the women were smarter and it was harder to believe that they actually showed an interest in you. Me. It was semicool to be broke, so there wasn't much pressure to actually go anywhere or do anything. So I did okay there, too, although the relationships lasted a little longer.

Dating after college sucked. Until Amy.

And it would have gotten worse. I have no illusions that there's some destiny girl out there who I didn't meet because of Amy. And no ideal woman who would have entered my life if I hadn't rebounded with Brin. No nubile grad student waiting to learn from the master. No braless pathfinder whose noble life was made nobler by my nearness to her side. No stripper would have ever gone back to my hotel unless I offered her a roll of singles big enough to . . . I don't know . . . big enough to . . .

I'm tired.

And nervous. Because I haven't had a first time with a woman in a long, long time.

Yeah, in theory, the idea of guilt-free sex with a hot hottie sounds great. On the other hand . . .

How the hell can there be another hand? We're talking guilt-free sex with a hot hottie.

But there is. There's another hand.

I don't know what it is, but I know there's another hand. There's a hand that's making Doug weirder and there's a hand that burst Randy's heart and there's a hand that's making Brin more secretive and there's a hand that's messing with my mind about Amy.

That's more than just another hand. That's lots of other hands. That's a goddamn Hindu god's worth of other hands.

But in the middle of the night, when I get up to go to the bathroom not because I need to go to the bathroom but because I've been up for an hour and when I get back to sleep I don't want to wake up before I have to because I actually do have to go to the bathroom, I've caught myself looking in the mirror and what I think is, "Don't pretend you have problems, you dick."

CHERYL

Hey Brin-ster. When we started walking together I bet you never thought one morning we'd go walking and the subject of our conversation would be the relative merits of the prostitute we interviewed. Me, I totally saw it coming. Somehow when I first met you I knew screening prostitutes was in our shared future. I'm very like Nostradamus in that and other respects. Other predictions: Someone in our little circle will someday become a professional stripper. I predict Doug. You should see him in pasties.

Ha, ha. Made you snort.

Hey, have I ever told you how glad I was when Martin married you? I was. Glad. Oh, I knew you'd make him happy and all that, but I didn't care about those things. I was happy for selfish reasons. My main concern after Martin split up with Amy was that when he got remarried—and I knew he'd get remarried, Martin just isn't somebody who stays single—that he choose a friend for me. I would have liked to have had veto power, really. Anytime I thought there was any danger of him going out with someone I couldn't be friends with, I'd do what I could to drive them away. Make casual offhand references in conversation to his freakishly tiny penis. Put up flyers on telephone poles accusing him of being a sexual predator. Talk about how much he likes Celine Dion's music. Whatever it took.

I called it the "Friend-for-Cheryl" program.

You should have seen us when we'd all get together. Because you know how Dierdre is, she's fantastic in an "I-like-baby-animals-and-angels" way, but she's kind of in her own little Dierdreworld anyway. And then there's Amy in her hard candy shell. There was no connecting and very little laughing.

So I was psyched when Martin married you. Because Amy was nice, but a little too nice, you know? Or rather: too nice on the outside, not nice enough on the inside? Kind of like a vinegar-chocolate truffle? I know she's smart, Martin wouldn't have married her if she wasn't, but she was one of those people who as soon as she had kids decided not to be that smart anymore. You know what I'm talking about? Like, motherhood is such a full and rewarding experience, why would anyone ever bother talking about anything else? That's one thing I kind of appreciate about Dierdre: I know she loves Ty but she always kind of acts like he's just this cool young person who happens to live in their house, rather than the center of her existence.

Plus, whenever I made a joke about, whatever, the Special Olympics or dead people, Amy would always give me this look. It was a very infuriating look. You don't have that look in your repertoire. Around you, I make a joke about double amputees, you're more likely to make one about quadruple amputees, and add on a quote from Jacques Derrida in French. I appreciate this in a person.

If you didn't make me take vigorous walks in the

morning, you'd be perfect. Oh, yeah, and if you hadn't jeopardized my marriage with elaborate lies and then dragged me into the illegal underworld of high-priced prostitution. Amy never would have done that. Other than these things, though, you're swell.

Why am I telling you this now? I'm not sure. I guess I figured that things are going to get crazier before they get saner and I want to make sure that you know you're golden.

MARTIN 244 POUNDS

Once the kids went to bed, I was going to give Amy a call, but Brin had picked up a movie from Blockbuster and it was already getting to that "too late to start the movie without serious risk of falling asleep during it" so I decided to wait.

"What do you think about getting a big-screen TV?" she asked.

"Sounds good to me," I told her, knowing that when she said something like that it meant that she had already done most of the shopping legwork.

DOUG 230 POUNDS

We used to hire people to do heavy chores in our yard: the leaves, shoveling the snow. I'd always thought it was because that was just the kind of people we are: the kind of people who hire other people to do the things we don't want to do. (Up to and including sleeping with me, apparently.)

Turns out that's not why we did it. Apparently we did it because Cheryl assumed if I did those chores I'd drop dead from a heart attack. For years she's thought of me as a great big blubbery china doll, teetering on the edge of mortality, about to keel over at any second if I engaged in the slightest physical exertion. Now that I've lost weight and am healthier, she's stopped hiring those neighborhood kids and I've had to do it. And you know what? Yard work blows.

I tried to use Randy's heart attack to scare her: Look, it could still happen. She wasn't buying it. Think she's looking at it like it's lightning: Randy got struck, so now Martin and I are statistically safer. So now this is how I'm spending my Saturdays—doing shit in the yard. I come in all gritty and sweaty and just really full of resentment.

"Is there any part of this weight-loss deal that doesn't fucking suck?" I said, stripping down for the shower.

"Well, the sex-with-a-prostitute part, I'm guessing," Cheryl said.

"Yeah," I said. "That part. That part really fucking rocks."

DIERDRE

Journal Entry #6

One thing I want to say, or, write, is that I like absolutely everything about journaling class except for the journaling. I hope that doesn't hurt your feelings or anything. I know we're supposed to write like nobody's ever going to read these except for us but I know you're going to, which is okay, fair, you're the teacher and how are you going to grade us if you don't look at our journals, it's a journaling class. What, are you going to grade our good intentions? And the honor system only goes so far, believe me, I could tell you some stories from high school but I won't right now because that seems like an awful lot of writing and I think my hand would start to hurt, besides it's kind of private, not sure it belongs in my personal journal. The teacher in my acting class says I have issues with trust but that's just because I won't do the trust falls everyone has to do, I explain that it's not that I don't trust everyone, it's just that they're going to drop me. Besides a person spends her whole life trying not to fall, I don't think it's a good use of my night school fees to start falling all over again. Don't get me started on bungee jumpers. Besides I do trust people, I trust Randy, I'd trust him to the end of the world. Couldn't ask him to do what I'm telling him to do if I didn't trust him, I can't say what, let's just say it's because he lost all this weight.

We're big into self-improvement. Used to trust Brin and Cheryl, too; still like them but trust not quite so much anymore, but that's kind of private. Let's just say that just because we were breaking the law together didn't mean to me that we could lie to each other and keep secrets and stuff, especially with regards to the law-breaking and the inventing of fake people and so forth. Yeah, really, actually I've got a whole lot going on in my life right now that I could write about, probably be pretty cool to write about it but, no, I don't think so, not for you, sorry, thanks anyway. I hope that doesn't hurt my grade.

How about this, if I just say this, that my friends and I are doing this thing where we're meeting a lot of really interesting and attractive people and it's maybe one of the most fun things I've ever done in my life. Let's just say it's kind of private and a little illegal and I know you can't say anything because of teacher-journal privilege, but I go to bed every night feeling really sexy, and how bad a thing can that be?

RANDY 212 POUNDS

I'm there.

Well, not there. Just a few missed meals away. Go figure, it was the heart attack diet that put me over the edge. Well, not over the edge. Not yet. Two pounds. Used to be really difficult to lose two pounds. Might be difficult to lose these two.

Don't think about it.

Don't think about it at all.

Don't think about the fact that I appear to be leaving Martin and Doug in the dust.

Don't think about the fact that I'm going to make love with another woman in the not-too-distant future.

DOUG 228 POUNDS

Randy's going to win. That bastard is going to take this and get the first roll in the hay with hooker woman.

Figures, the ex-athlete takes it. Bastards like him won everything in high school. Won everything in college. Even when they turn into fat fuckers, they win everything. Figures he'd be the lucky asshole who got to have the heart attack.

MARTIN 230 POUNDS

I can do this. Stay motivated. Get on the bike. Park at the back of the lot. Guzzle Diet Coke. Complete what I started. Show Brin the guy I used to be. The one who Amy loved. The one who saw his kids every morning and every night. The one who had it and blew it.

I can do this.

DOUG 219 POUNDS

What if I just stopped? Stopped here, a perfectly respectable weight, I've mostly won the game but I don't have to sleep with this woman? That would prove something, wouldn't it? Like the guy who runs all the way to the finish line to prove he can win the race, then stops and lets other people cross the line first because he doesn't have to win?

(Who am I thinking of? Isn't there someone, in a movie or something, who does something like that? And if so, why? Stupid asshole, just cross the finish line. Perhaps not the best example for me to follow.)

Because these last nine pounds seem like they're going to be a lot of work. And sleeping with this woman, like a little boy taking Mommy's reward for being a good trooper, seems like more work. Let Martin and fucking Randy take the prize and look at me and wonder why I seem so strangely superior. It's good to be inscrutable, right?

Problem is, you know I won't stay at 219 forever. We all know this, surely. I'm a slave to my fucking appetites, for Christ's sake, and hovering around 219 seems almost as difficult as getting down to 210. If I hover at 219, I'm doing a lot of work for nothing, which makes me the chump and the other guys the winners. And if I get fat again, then it's like I couldn't cut it, which makes me the loser and the other guys the winners. And if I noticeably stop trying to win the prize, we're back to Cheryl getting suspicious of me, which she will.

Fuck!

Fine, fine, I'll put down the fucking Dove bar.

To: BrinM@compumail.net
From: Chercher@worknet.com
Subject: The lucky girl

B,

You have the honor of being about to read the weirdest
e-mail I've ever composed.

Of all the candidates we interviewed I think Cinnamon's the
front-runner. She seemed professional and serious and
straightforward. None of which is particularly sexy, but I think
that's one of the things I like. But she does look good. Which
is, of course, necessary. And she kind of sort of looks like
she might possibly be the woman in that picture we showed
the guys. If you squint at her. In the dark. And you're drunk.

Dierdre stopped by my place this morning on her way to
her scrapbooking class and she dropped off her notes about
the interviews. She wrote about eight or nine pages about
each woman, and the whole thing reads like breathless les-
bian erotica. Randy is one lucky bastard to have this gal
looking after him. After having read her notes, and subse-
quently toweled off, I infer that she prefers Cinnamon as well.
She doesn't say so explicitly, but Cinnamon seems to get
more adjectives than the others.

Shall we schedule a meeting, my evil genius?

Loveyameanit,

C.

MARTIN 222 POUNDS

I've practically stopped eating. I don't ingest Listerine strips any more because of their calories. When I'm home I weigh myself every twenty minutes. I catch myself shooting warm and longing looks at the toilet, flashing back to that discussion we all had about throwing up and thinking if it was good enough for the Romans . . .

I'm screwed up. I'm like a fifteen-year-old girl in an after-school special. This is the problem with this goal-oriented plan, with hanging everything on the peg of this target weight. The closer I get, the less mentally healthy I become. The rumbling void in my stomach at bedtime is like a treasured friend; I love it more than my wife or offspring. I surf for pictures of food on the Internet at work, and it's an acceptable substitute for actually eating it. I used to think Nigella Lawson was a hottie. Now I think her chicken breasts are sexier, and at the same time I loathe her for liking to eat too much.

This has to end soon. No more food. Period.

BRIN

Here's something that needs to be spelled out, I think. We need you to pretend to be someone. Can you do that? No, I can tell by the way you say "sure" that you don't fully understand what I mean. I know you probably pretend to be people all the time. Teachers, meter maids, someone's boss, whatever. I'm not talking about, whatever, mutual willing suspension of disbelief. It's not like he's the escaped convict and you're the warden's wife, no offense if you've ever done time, or no offense that I just said *that* if you've never done time. It's not a role-playing thing, is what I'm saying, where you both play the game and then drop it when it comes time to settle up and leave or whatever. You're not pretending to be someone else for his, uh, gratification. We want you to fool him. All three of them. Make him think you're someone else. Someone I went to school with. Your real name is Missy Paterson, you went to Cedar College, you majored in psychology, graduated in 1992, we were friends, hung out together, fell out of touch after college, your career took an unexpected turn. You see what I mean?

I don't mean to be obnoxious but I'm not sure by the way you say "sure" that we're on the same page. I'm belaboring this only because it occurs to me that this is probably somewhat unusual. You probably don't have very many clients who want you actually to deceive or confuse them. I mean—*they* don't want you to deceive them, *we* want you to deceive them. Is that okay? I mean, that doesn't go against any, whatever, professional code or something like that? I wouldn't want you to get, whatever, disbarred or—you know what I mean, reprimanded or suspended—okay, I can tell by the way you're smiling that you're laughing at me, which is fair enough, even as I said those things I realized how stupid they were, I'm not that naive. Dierdre is actually the naive one. (Sorry, Dierdre, I forgot you were still here, I'll apologize to you later.)

Also, it would be good if you could look as much like the woman in this picture as possible.

So can you do that? Pretend you're someone else? I realize it might not come up, but some of these guys are chatty, they might make small talk, ask you about me, about school, whatever. While they're taking off their pants, or whatever, they might be nervous, or curious, or just a little annoying—a couple of these guys can be pretty annoying. (See, Cheryl's nodding, she agrees with me.) So have you ever done any acting? I mean—of course you have, sure. But—I suppose it's too much to ask that you've ever taken any psychology classes. We could change your major but I think I might already have said something about psychology. I probably have an old textbook around I could lend you, just drop some terminology if it comes up—"transference" or "projection." Might want to avoid stuff like "Oedipal" or "performance anxiety" but that's your call, you're the professional. I just don't want you to get into a situation where you feel—sorry? Oh, good, you have. How many classes? Well, huh. Phi Beta Kappa, no kidding. I don't mean to act surprised, no. I think it's great that you have a master's. You're very—no, I could tell you were bright. "Educated," yes, that's what I meant to say. So we—sorry? About me? Sure, you should probably know a few things about me, to share in case of—well, I don't think they'll be asking about my GPA. No, don't worry about that, if you just know that I had a couple of bad semesters that were beyond my control that's probably—. I don't remember. I'm professionally successful now, that's what's important, you know how that is, you're professionally successful as well, we're both . . . Anyway, I think that's all we have to share right now, Cheryl? Dierdre? Yeah, see, that's it, so—. No, that's good. You're set. That's fine.

CINNAMON

People who like to pretend to be enlightened and frank and nonjudgmental will always ask questions, acting interested, we're all adults here so here are some questions about your job but what they don't realize from my standpoint is that if you really think about it no one's really that curious about anyone else's job. I don't ask you about your data processing and you don't ask him about real estate developing and he doesn't ask her about the travel agency, and work's just what we all do because we have to do it, no one wants to talk about it, so when you ask me about it acting like it's just normal nonexotic adult conversation what you're really doing is telling me how abnormal exotic and juvenile you think my work is.

Just let me talk about it a little while. You'll see how boring my job is.

Lots of times the questions, even though no one would ever say this, boil down to: Isn't it awful? Isn't your job, you know, awful? Which is probably what the subtext would be of every conversation you ever had about other people's jobs if you ever talked about other people's jobs, which you don't, because they're all awful.

Most parts of most people's jobs are awful, and it's the same with mine. But not the parts these three women think. These three women who interviewed me for this gig think the parts of my job that are unspeakably awful involve the men in the bed. As though their sex lives with their husbands aren't transactions. As if they don't go into every sex act with some combination of expectations, obligation, submission, demands, revulsion, and ritual. As if the most important part of the sex were the sex itself rather than something else it represents. The only difference between the sex I have and the sex most people have is I have more of it.

That class I took in semiotics would probably have something to say about this. These women probably think semiotics is what I have to wash out of my skirt after a gig. Maybe not the one in the middle. She's got that big-frontal-lobe 'tude about her, like she's way too smart for her haircut. Gotta like that.

Revelation. Sex isn't the worst part of my job. The worst part is this part. The negotiation. The conversation. The "what-if-I-want-to-do-this?" The "have-you-ever-been-asked-to-do-that?" The "I-bet-you've-never-been-asked-this-question-before."

That's the part of the pretending I hate the most. "This is going to be a new one." "I'm not like most of your clients." "Hold on to your hat." Like these women, sitting in a row of dining-room-set chairs, the way they keep looking at me waiting for me to do a double take. "You want me to whaaaa? I've never heard of anything like that before!" Because they don't realize there are wives who give this to their husbands for anniversary presents. Wives who give it to their husbands just to get them out of the house for a while. The one who gave it to her husband for running the Chicago Marathon. The one who gave it so he'd start cleaning the toilets. He traded ten minutes with me for a lifetime of Clorox. I would have advised him differently.

Even when it's just the guy, you always have to play the game. Guys are always like "This is going to sound weird but," or "I'm a little unusual because." No one knows they're pretty much like everybody else. No one wants to know. Job starts a long time before we're in a room with a bed in it. Got to make them feel like they're a certain kind of person, make them think they're something they're not, make them think you're responding to them one way when you're responding another way. Everyone knows you do that while you're doing it, no one realizes you're doing it when you first meet them. These three women want to be the most eccentric most unusual suburban women I've ever met, people who would shock the socks off the other mothers in the play group, who'd make the other guys on the street drop their jaws. Okay. I give them that. Never heard of anything like this before. Gosh I don't know, I guess that's okay. You guys are really out there, but sure. Pretend to be someone you knew in college well wow that's kind of weird but sure I guess I can do that you're the client after all and the customer's always right I guess I could do my hair different and talk about certain things and pretend to have a different past and act like I'm somebody I'm not I suppose I could rise to the task given that's only something I do every single day and six times on a good Saturday yeah sure why not I'll give it a shot! But maybe we could talk about it a while longer first, maybe you guys could shoot looks at each other a few more times like you're the first men on Uranus or maybe I could answer a few more questions from your word-processed questionnaires or maybe I could talk a little bit more about the ways I am or am not at all what you expected, I could pretend that I wish someone would write me a love letter or the first boy I ever liked and how it never entered my head what kissing meant till he put his tongue in my mouth or I could show you how easy it is to draw a line from a philosophy major at a private college to what I'm doing now and how the steps from point A to point Z are as simple and unrelated and inevitable as a PowerPoint presentation, that's what scares you the one on the left, I can tell by the way you keep squinting at me that you're worried at how easily we might have traded places at some point, or I could talk some more about the wives and girlfriends who get in on the sessions with me and the client, because that's what interests the one on the right, she's cute and sexy and flirty and she keeps looking at my neck wondering if there's any way she can justify getting back in touch with me later for a little one-on-one, or I could just keep answering questions no one needs to hear the answers to because that's what the one in the middle wants, because there's a sense that if this conversation takes a certain form and fills up a certain length of time then she's done her job and struck just the right balance between depravity and normalcy or I could talk about how I never would have chosen this color carpet and how I believe wall-to-wall carpet is an atrocity anyway or hey on the other hand here's a wild idea what

the high-impact infidelity diet

if we just agree on the times and the places yes and stop talking to each other because I have dry cleaning to pick up yes and an overdue Mark Wahlberg movie to return yes and it's my day for car pool yes plus I have a date tonight and I thought there was something else oh yes there's also the small niggling fact that I've already said yes I'll do it yes I will Yes.

Thought I'd never get out of there.

DOUG 217 POUNDS

I don't even know the guy, but it's one in the morning at the hotel bar and there's nothing there—nothing—worth even shooting for. He must have sensed that I was doing a last check for the same thing he was and he starts talking to me about stuff that happened on the trade show floor and ways that the registration people screwed up with some new computer system and then he says a couple of things about the tail that was trolling around and he's got sweatshirts that he's only supposed to give to potential big-order customers but how he always gives them to the hotties. I tell him enough so he knows I'm straight and he tells me that this town's terrible on strip clubs but he was here last year and there's a nice little house just a short cab ride from the hotel.

What I want to tell him is that I'll pass because my wife has already arranged for me to get some pay-for-play action. "Yeah," I'd tell him, "my wife. She set me up. Paid for it out of her own bank account and everything."

"Where do I get a wife like that?" he'd ask.

And I'd smile because, you know, when you think about it, it's damn cool of Cheryl to let all of this happen. Damn cool of her.

The house turns out to be a little on the dumpy side. The bar dude must be a pretty good salesman because he threatens to walk away if he doesn't get his price.

There are only two girls and one is kind of ugly, so I read some old *Newsweek*s while I wait for the other guy to finish. Ugly girl doesn't seem to mind that I'm waiting. If I was in a better mood, I'd at least talk to her. In the middle of things, I think I hear a baby crying somewhere else in the house, but I could be wrong.

When I finish the deed (B+ for effort, C– for creativity, no curve) and come back to the front room, bar guy is gone but the bill is paid. I leave a good tip and borrow the phone to get a cab. I try not to read into the dispatcher's tone or talk to the driver while she takes me back to the Hilton.

BRIN

Well, Cheryl. This hasn't been weird at all, has it? When you think about it? It's just like hiring a nanny, I assume. When you think about it. Like hiring a contractor to work on your house. If that contractor were going to, say, fellate your husband instead of expanding your kitchen.

See, not weird at all. When you think about it. Which one of these is your coffee? That doesn't help me, I never know whether venti is bigger than grande or vice versa. It's like the frigging metric system in here.

I wish I had Dierdre's joie de vivre about the whole thing. She's enjoyed the whole process arguably too much. She didn't even stay that mad at us about the lying thing. Maybe she just can't stay mad, period. Mad just slides right off her. Right, she's like the anti-Doug.

Incidentally, I'm assuming you completely noticed the way the barista was utterly macking on you, yes? Barista— the guy making the coffee, aren't they called baristas? He was. Oh yes he was. Yeah, he was. He completely was. He was. He was. Well, no, not now, he has other customers. But when you ordered, he was all over you. He was. I'm serious, Cheryl. He thoroughly dug you. He did. He made that joke, when you ordered? I know, but I think it was supposed to be a joke. I know, it's cute.

I don't know why guys didn't hit on you like that in college. Since I wasn't there, I can't even confirm that they didn't. Based on your cluelessness today, I'm guessing they did and you had no idea. Knowledge is fun, no?

Oh, stop. He's maybe twenty-two, that guy. He's got all that hair. You'd never—you'd be a weird couple, first of all. And you know how much you hate the way Doug mumbles? That guy has so many piercings in his lip that he's physically incapable of enunciation. He'd be a bad match for you. Oh, a torrid affair, sure. A roll in the hay from which you'd emerge smelling like Sumatran dark roast and patchouli? I could completely see that. I'd encourage it. I'd celebrate it. What the hell, you know? You wouldn't have to end up like Emma Bovary.

Me? No, no. I could never do it. First, baristas are never into me. Second, I don't do "torrid." I'd prefer to live vicariously through your imagined affairs.

You know? For a couple of broads who just hired a prostitute, we are mighty lame.

RANDY 211 POUNDS

Parent-teacher conferences are never as fun as I think they're going to be. When I was a kid I imagined they were way too cool, these two parts of my life coming together, my mom and my teacher in the same room together, just something kind of exciting about that I guess because it didn't usually happen. It was like a crossover episode, like when Mork or Laverne would show up on *Happy Days*. Plus there was always the chance that my mom might make my teacher cry, which I thought I might find out about later.

Turns out, parent-teacher conferences? They're not that cool. Not even that useful, frankly. Maybe they're useful for some kids, the really bad ones or maybe the really good ones, but Ty is, I guess, kind of like I was: neither of those but something in between. And it always seems like his teacher is working really hard to try and find words to describe him, like if the adjectives are good enough we'll think we're getting our tax money's worth. They should get a calendar like mine, these teachers. "Your son is really emblematic." "Ty is just so solipsistic." Wouldn't mean anything but at least it would be more interesting than the conferences we have now, which also don't mean anything.

This one was a little different in the sense that Ty's teacher this year, Ms. Krohn, is really really hot. And she has this great long black hair, so black it looks blue, and nice hands and great legs, which she kept crossing and uncrossing in her short skirt so that frankly I don't even know what adjectives she ended up making up about Ty, I just wanted to stay in the conference as long as possible. Which we did, because Dierdre kept asking questions. Which is very unusual, because she doesn't usually ask questions at these things, but she kept saying stuff like "Could you tell us more?" and "What else should we know?" so that I totally had maximum exposure to Ms. Krohn and her hair and her hands and her legs until after the conference I was actually a little worried about standing up without being too, uh, prominent.

Dierdre must have sensed it or been in the mood anyway or something because we went straight out to the school parking lot and had sex there in the front seat, which is probably against all sorts of laws but it's my first front-seat sex experience and I'm definitely not complaining.

I am kind of wishing though that Brin's college friend looked more like Ms. Krohn. Oh well. Shouldn't be greedy.

MARTIN 215 POUNDS

I wonder how long it would take for me to gain all the weight back if I really tried.

I mean, let's say Brin said to me, "If you get back up to 250, you can have a threesome. . . ."

CHERYL

Hey, Dierdre. What are you doing? Grocery shopping, sure, obviously, me too. Don't you hate grocery shopping? Really? Huh. No, I do, I hate it. Usually I make Doug do it. Yeah, but I just thought—I don't know, he's lost all this weight for me, or okay, for his penis but because of me, directly or indirectly, plus he's doing more chores around the house, I thought maybe the least I could do is do more of the grocery shopping.

Not to mention it's probably good for me to know how one of these so-called grocery stores works, right? I mean, what if Doug and I . . . I mean . . . what if Doug got hit by a bus? Or crushed by falling satellite debris? Or lost all his limbs in a freak office-supplies accident? I'd need to—I'd need to step up, wouldn't I? These are the things I think about.

Plus, as long as Doug did all the shopping, I never knew one could get ketchup without mesquite flavoring or habanero peppers in it. The things one learns, ha-ha.

Cereal? It's aisle seven. I know that aisle well.

Yeah. We like cereal, too. We used to have a wall of breakfast cereal in the house—although we never really bought into the "breakfast" part. Cereal was an important part of our diet. In the morning, yes, but also before bed, sometimes as a dinner replacement. In front of *Oprah*. Not just grown-up cereals. Doug would come back from the supermarket and every box of cereal would have a cartoon character on it. He particularly liked the limited-edition ones. He stockpiled Kellogg's Homer Simpson's Cinnamon Donut Cereal knowing that, at some point in the not-so-distant future, it would disappear, never to be heard from again. We had a crate in the garage for all of the toys that came in the cereal boxes and we'd mix them up with the candy we gave out on Halloween. Kids loved our house. We never got egged.

That your grocery list? Oh, I see, it's like a bullet-point list only instead of bullet points you use little flowers. And happy faces. That's very organized. And very Prozac.

Anyway, when this whole contest thing began, we got rid of the cereals. Now I miss them. I'm sick of cereals with athletes or numbers on the front and only nutritional information to read on the back. Dammit, when I'm eating cereal, I want to do a maze or find a hidden Cap'n Crunch. Is that so wrong? Hell, I wish other food was packaged like that. I wish risotto came with a word jumble and pictures of cartoon pirates. Or Italians. Whatever.

Doug seems cured of his cereal addiction. I'm not. Which is why—confession time, you ready?—the other morning, I took a big Tupperware bowl with me out of the house. And I took a spoon. And I came to this very grocery store even though we didn't need any groceries then and I picked up a half gallon of milk and a box of Fruity Pebbles. And anybody who walked by could have seen me sitting at the far corner of the supermarket parking lot, filling the bowl over and over and over again, and wondering what's going to happen. To me. To Doug. To Doug and me.

You know?

Do you have to go? Yoga class, sure, I understand. Insofar as—I mean, I don't understand why anyone takes yoga class, but I understand why you have to go. Or rather, why you're saying you'd have to go; I'd totally say the same thing if I were you. See you later, Dierdre. Good to see you, Dierdre. Enjoy your cereal, Dierdre.

RANDY 211 POUNDS

Dierdre had a good point, she pointed out I should maybe want to go off my medication for a while. Not the heart stuff, the other stuff. The whatchacall. For my thing. What is it, I've got? The span. Not C-Span. What'sitcalled. Attention span. At least until after I have my, whatever, my session, my reward with the woman, because of the fact that side effects of the medication are supposed to possibly include, um, erectile badness, and maybe in a situation like this I don't need any obstacles. I should just get over my shyness and go fill that prescription for Dr. DePaulo's magic erecting pills. I don't even know for sure if that erectile side effect happens to me with the span pills or not, though it's true that since I got into my thirties Little Joe's been slower to get up to the plate, takes longer to slide into home, and every once in a while gets distracted around second base and lies down to take a nap in the outfield.

I barely notice because Dierdre's so patient and nice and so good about paying lots of attention to me but this woman might not feel like taking that time. She doesn't know me or Little Joe. On the one hand she's being paid— on some kind of alumni sisterhood discount, I hope—to do whatever I want so it shouldn't be a big deal, I'm sure she's asked to do weirder or more annoying things like call a guy "Daddy" or dress up like a big furry duck or change someone's diapers or other things like I've seen on HBO documentaries late at night; there are some weird people out there, I never would have guessed, and now they're all able to find each other thanks to the Internet, I guess; what must it have been like for those people before the Internet, to think you're the only person in the world who's into clown suits or giant plush dolls or women with hairy arms, can you imagine, sitting there in Sioux City or Tallahassee feeling all alone and ashamed and keeping everything to yourself and the only way you can get excited is by imagining to yourself that your date is wearing a Bozo wig or something?

Now it's all different, now it's people like me who feel weird and different, is there something wrong with me that I'm happy with pretty women with big chests and little waists and doing it face-to-face is fine with me? Makes me feel like I'm missing out on something, what do all these other people know that I don't? Columnists on the subject tell people to "experiment" but I wouldn't know where to start, how do you experiment when you don't even know where to start? It's so hit-and-miss. "Hold still, Dee, I'm going to write on you with lipstick. Hang on a second while I stick my thing into this acorn squash. Let's try it without taking our shoes off, maybe that'll click." Where do you start? I don't get it. I'm willing to try. But before I experiment I need some, what's the word, oh, heck, I can't think of the word I'm trying to think of, where's my calendar, I need some parameters. (That's the word. This calendar is awesome.)

Maybe this woman might have some suggestions, I could ask her after, small talk while I'm putting my socks back on. Or before, then she could make recommendations, like a waiter at a new restaurant, and I could try some things. One from column A, two from column B. Maybe she'll have a kit, like a doctor, basics for emergencies, a little black case with a feather and handcuffs and a jar of mustard. "Break glass in case of vanilla guy who doesn't know what he's talking about." Vanilla, that's what they call, like, people like me. Which makes sense. I really like vanilla. Ice cream. Cake. Ice cream cake. Pudding. Oh, sure, I'll have a bar of chocolate before I have a bar of vanilla, but when it comes to the flavoring of something—not chocolate or vanilla as a noun but as an adjective—then I'm vanilla all the way.

And I've never dated a black girl, although I think I'll go to my grave regretting not having done that. Is that racist?

I should be an easy client, I think. Not too many demands. Of course, I don't know, I'm so used to Dierdre, she's so sexy she makes it easy and, like I said before, she pays so much attention to me. I wonder if I should be wondering if that's satisfactory for her? Sometimes it seems like I barely do any touching of her at all. It's all me. Aren't women supposed to be all into foreplay? Maybe the prostitute could tell me. She's being paid, she can answer my questions if I want her to. I assume Dierdre's satisfied. Surely she'd say something otherwise. But then we don't talk. I mean, not about stuff like that, just about normal stuff. Stuff like TV and the lawn and the neighbors and potholes and Robert De Niro. She might not even know she's the only woman I've ever slept with. I wonder.

Anyway I think going off my medication is a good idea, Dierdre thinks so too, I don't think it'll even have any effect on me anyhow, I've probably grown out of it anyhow, Dierdre thinks so too, I'd really like to eat some cheese right now, that sounds good. Dierdre's being so great about all this, encouraging me to go off my medication even though I didn't even mention I was anxious about that, it's like she can read my mind as usual, like a magician or a, whatchacall, a prognosticator? Encouraging me to get a haircut. Buying me a new shirt, some pants. Again, this woman, she's paid, it's not like I have to impress her, I could go in without showering if I wanted (maybe that's something else some people like I wonder, dirty sex, not "dirty" but really dirty? Is that hot? Seems gross) or wearing something ugly like my Milwaukee's Best T-shirt or my sweatpants, but Dierdre and I are on the same page, I don't want to do anything like that, reflects poorly on me, it's like cleaning up your house before the maid comes. Maid outfits, that's probably something else people like, a girl in a maid outfit, or maybe the guy wears the maid outfit, either way I don't see the appeal, I'd be stressed out that she'd see a dust bunny and get distracted, besides it would make me think of *Hazel,* remember that show? That was a good show, that and *Bewitched. Sanford and Son* had a good theme song. Julie your cruise director was cute. *High Incident,* they canceled that show too soon. I think girls in cop uniforms are sexy, maybe she, the woman, could wear a cop uniform. No, that's probably illegal. Or just confusing. What if she was actually an undercover cop? Are you still an undercover cop if you are pretending to be a hooker who dresses like a cop? What if we're about to get going and she says, "Freeze, buddy, you're under arrest" and starts reading me my Miranda rights? How would I know if that was part of the act or if I was actually being busted. We could actually get busted. This is, after all, still illegal. We're breaking laws. But if Brin gave her the money, how am I guilty of anything? I'm just having sex with a woman who might or might not be dressed as a cop. I'm not paying her although a third of the money can surely be traced to my bank account. If there are receipts. I can't believe we don't have any cheese in the house. Ooh, look, a *TV Guide*.

MARTIN 210 POUNDS

In the first few years of my marriage to Amy, I used to take a condom with me whenever I went on a solo business trip.

There was always a semielaborate process in getting it out the door because I imagined Amy would do a last-minute clothing check in my suitcase (she was great that way—before we went to Barbados she noticed I didn't pack underwear or a razor) and find it there. Or she'd look in my wallet to get some money and find it there or pat me on the ass and there the disc would be. What I did was, at the last possible moment, I put it in the pocket of a pair of jeans I was packing, zip it into the suitcase, and try not to let go of the thing until I was safely in the car.

I never used it, but I'm not sure if that's the relevant moral issue. I had it, figuring that if I was going to cheat, at least I wouldn't bring home anything contagious.

The last time I took a condom on a business trip was in 1996 when I had to go to work a college recruitment fair up in Minneapolis. There was the usual dinner and shmoozing and the empty hotel room always inspired fantasies of late-night hotel bar conquests—never with anyone I was working with, that would be too dangerous. It was always—in theory—some initiative-grabbing woman at the bar, drunk enough to be forward but not so drunk that I felt like I was taking advantage. This imaginary woman knew what she wanted and she didn't give a damn if I was married and she told me straight out not to like her too much because this, sir, was a one-night stand and if I wanted anything different, I should look elsewhere. No phone number. No last name unless it's on the badge that she forgot to take off.

That woman and I never met. I knew she was in the hotel somewhere, but I either got to the bar too late or she checked out early or she decided to pull a Mrs. Robinson on a handsome young coworker. Sometimes she was at the bar, but she just hadn't had enough drinks to be forward. And the thought of my actually initiating a conversation with her—knowing full well my intention of going down the path to adultery—even two-states-away adultery—seemed pathetic.

So I invariably had a drink or two and went back to my room to fall asleep to another HBO movie. If I was lucky, it would be rated TV-MA.

This one time, though, I had had a great day—a killer day—when I was at the top of my business guy game. Everything I said was witty or insightful. I could practically see my out-of-town associates wishing for a pen to jot down my bon mots and words of wisdom in order to share them later with loved ones and lesser coworkers. Stunned, they were and I was so damn cool about it—like some Hollywood cover girl pretending she didn't understand why everyone thought she was so beautiful—that it made me even sharper. I don't get days like that too often, but sometimes they happen and they convince you, at least for a few hours, that you are exactly where you should be—that life has taken you to a place where you are the exact person for the job. That was me that day.

I was high from that—and a couple of gimlets over the course of dinner—but right after dessert everyone left and I was alone with my brilliant self.

When you are in the state where planets seem to be orbiting around you, you should not be left by yourself.

I tried to accept this abandonment—I watched a movie on HBO in the room, then watched another movie on HBO. Then I was feeling a little hungry, or pretending that I was hungry—I was so busy being pithy at dinner I had barely eaten, right?—and opted to enter the world beyond the hotel.

In the rental car, I realized that I hadn't asked the concierge for restaurant recommendations and didn't know the territory, so I wasn't going to stray too far from the major streets. I could have opted for the TGI Friday's next to the hotel but that just wasn't where I wanted to be.

A few minutes of four-lane led to what passed for a downtown. Dead this late, except for a neighborhood bar and I'm always suspicious of neighborhood bars that don't seem to have a neighborhood around them. Downtown is never the place for a late stop anyway so I kept moving, figuring I'd give it another two miles or so before turning back to a Friday's fallback.

A few auto dealers later, though, I saw the neon lights of a strip club. I don't remember the name of it, to be honest, or even what the sign looked like but I'm sure it involved a pair of legs in the air. So there might have been a V in the name.

I drove past the club's valet station and, without really making a conscious decision to do it, turned the corner. It's not like I was thinking "they might have food" and it's not like I was thinking, "I'm in the mood to see naked women." I just turned the corner and parked and paid the $6 cover and chose the bar instead of a ringside seat and ordered a beer (another $6, which seemed to be the number of choice here since it left the maximum number of singles in change).

Before I even got the lay of the land, there was a woman on the next barstool. Unlike the heavy-breasted woman onstage, she was clothed—big heels, white shirt, short shorts, a tie, heavy-framed black glasses: the complete intellectual hottie outfit—and I was amazed at how I hadn't seen her approach. I knew the stool was empty when I sat down. It's not like the club was that dark.

She started talking right away. Not brashly and not pretend seductively—more like my buddy from college. She didn't really look at me right away—although I guessed that she had sized me up as I walked in. She watched the strippers up on the stage and I tried to, too, but I couldn't take my eyes away from her for long. Maybe, I realize now, that's why she looked away, to give me time to soak her in. Long black hair. Vaguely half-ethnic look (Sicilian? Indian? Egyptian?) but with a clearly New York voice (in a good way). She complained about her feet. She stretched as if it had been a long night. She asked me my name and I told her the truth—first name only, of course—and when I asked her hers, she said "Debbie—although here I'm Kim." She asked me about my day and gently questioned about how long I was in town and where I was from and whether I was alone and how often I came to town on business. She wanted to know how my shirt sleeve got torn and I hadn't noticed that my shirt sleeve was torn and she asked if I needed a sewing kit and the thought of me sitting at a strip club with a needle and thread made both of us laugh in a way that seemed to shatter all the pretense and cliché of the situation.

Gone.

Now it was two people who'd gotten a kick out of each other having a conversation. She asked if I'd ever been to the club before. I said no, I was just out looking for some food and she had the bartender get me a menu, which he did, but the prices were as steep as the drinks and when she asked if I was going to get anything I said, no, I'd rather save the money for her.

That's when I first noticed her looking at me.

And when I knew I had her.

I didn't intend to hook her with that. I was just being honest. But I felt something there, something building off that moment of connection over the sewing, and I realized that my marriage hadn't rendered moot my ability to catch the attention of a beautiful woman. I hadn't lost that piece of me.

Not that I was ever convinced I had it. I still remember the moment when I realized that Amy was in love with me. I already knew I was head over heels for her but I didn't want to tip that hand too soon. She was just amazingly funny and warm and smart and had her shit together in a way that made me feel half the time like I was interviewing her—I just wanted to hear her take on everything. Inevitably her comments would be smart or funny or insightful or reveal the heart of a situation in a way that opened up windows on everything. And her hair, it was longer then, always was just a little messy, which, I hadn't realized until I met Amy, was a major, major turn-on.

"That's really sweet," said the stripper who I really wasn't thinking of as a stripper yet because she hadn't taken off anything, "but you should really eat if you're hungry."

I told her I wasn't and she asked if I wanted to "go for a dance," which meant take a trip into the side room for lap fun.

"Not yet," I said and then told her that there were naked women all over the club but I couldn't take my eyes off her. Out loud I articulated my amazement at attraction. How it's amazing how someone can be attracted to one person and not another and how, for someone else, it might be the opposite. Debbie/Kim was not just beautiful. She had something else, too, that I couldn't describe. I was honest with her. Honest in my amazement. Honest in being unable to figure out how and why I was attracted to the women I was drawn to.

I told her that no matter what happened, she was going to get whatever money was in my wallet. I was being honest there, too. I knew I was sitting on about $45, which I'm sure isn't much as far as these things go. But maybe it is. What do I know? Maybe I was the best prospect there right now. Maybe she knew that when I came in. Or maybe, like with waitresses, I just happened to land at her station.

No, there was something else. She was waiting for me. Someone like me. Someone who wasn't just there to fulfill some fantasy of his. Someone who saw her for who she was and could make her laugh and find out what she needed to take her burden away. She touched my knee when she laughed. She didn't leave it there too long and she didn't pull it away awkwardly. She just touched my knee.

I told her that I was in room 215 of the Ramada Inn and that, if she came by after work, I would give her the body massage of her life.

I told her that she probably heard lines like that all the time but that I was making that offer with no expectations of what would happen and no strings. That I just wanted to return to her some of the pleasure that she gave me just by being so beautiful. That, too, was honest, because I wasn't thinking about screwing her. Maybe I would massage her and she would fall asleep in my hotel bed and I would stare at her all night long, marveling. The thought of kneading her body and hearing purrs of contentment—not fake purrs but real, involuntary purrs—

would have been enough of a thrill. It was an amazing body, although really the only skin I could see was her legs (which had brushed against mine a few times in our conversation) and hands (which had touched mine a few times as well to punctuate her comments). But there were other women—the one onstage, for instance, and the one sitting on the guy at the table in front of me— with made-for-pornography hard bodies. Saying I wasn't just interested in her looks seems insincere but, god-damn it, I wasn't just interested in her looks.

I told her that I understood why she would be reluc-tant but that passing up opportunities in life does not lead to a very interesting life.

I told her that the hotel was right down the road.

I told her that not only would she get a nice night's sleep, but that she could enjoy the complimentary buffet breakfast the next morning.

She smiled and it was a sincere smile and for the first time—and I mean this—it occurred to me that this could actually turn into wall-slamming, bed-breaking, fantasy-fuel-to-carry-me-to-retirement sex (after all, I had a condom).

She commented on how sweet that was and how she could really use the massage and how the feet and legs sounded good but she had a thing against getting her back rubbed. I theorized that that could be because so many guys use the back rub thing as a come-on and just give a cursory rub so that they could quickly move on to the next level (why the hell I thought I knew how other guys operate, I don't know) and she agreed that that might be part of it but it was also that her grandmother used to rub her shoulders after high school basketball practice and her grandmother had somehow gotten it into her head that rough equals good when it comes to massaging. I assured her that that was not my philosophy and took the sign that she was telling me about her grandmother as an indication that she was more comfortable with me than she'd been with any man for a very, very long time.

Part of any successful business deal is knowing when to leave. If you can leave the table at the point where the other person most wants to do business with you, you have the best chance of making things work out your way. So I told her that I didn't want to monopolize her time (showing you have the other party's best interest in mind is useful, too) and that she could make a lot more money if I wasn't around. She sighed and smiled and I was hit again with the sense that my humanitarianism was winning big points as she led me by the hand around the stage and up the few stairs, past a bouncer, and into the lap dancing area, where I gave her a twenty and asked if that was acceptable and she proceeded to kick off those painful-looking shoes and give me close-up access to everything that the law and the bouncers would allow, constantly writhing and changing positions to keep me from locking in on any one part of her. I had guessed small, sharpish nipples but hers were big and there was, in this light, a blemish just to the right of her chin that I wanted to see more clearly because it made her even more amazing to watch.

I wasn't sure of the what-my-hands-were-allowed-to-do protocol, but I didn't do anything that caused her to stop me. I did rub her thighs while she sat on my lap facing over the wall at the stage and I did dig my thumbs into her heels (a technique that Amy never cared for but that Brin now loves) and she responded with that involuntary purr that sounded exactly like the one I had imagined I wouldn't hear until later. I started to rub her back, too, but quickly remembered and said some "oops" equivalent and she said "that's okay" while she slid down further and all I saw was her hair between my legs.

The song, which I hadn't been aware of, wound down and she got up and gave me a kiss on the cheek and I fought the temptation to hold her close. Instead, I took a breath and stood up, taking a pair of fives from my wallet and telling her that what just happened was sweet. She looked surprised at the extra ten and said, "sit down," which I did and she sat on my lap and played with my hair and shook her head, smiling.

"What's my room number?" I asked.

"215," she said, without hesitation.

"What do you think?" I locked into her eyes. Sincere.

"That felt really good," she said.

"In 215," I said, "it will all be about you."

"Can I wait to make a decision until you're ready to leave?"

"I'm leaving now."

Leave 'em wanting more.

"Oh. . . ."

And we were up and back into the main bar area and she said, "I have to think about it. I have to be careful."

And I said, "I understand that. But seriously think about it."

And I left.

And on the way out I realized that I still had money in my wallet even though I had told her that I was going to give her what was in there. And I felt dishonest but didn't want to go back in because there was a good chance I'd be seeing her soon, although I'd feel strange giving her money in the room because that would make her a prostitute and we never talked about exchanging money for the pleasure of her company.

There were fewer cars on the street now, although two guys were getting high in the car parked behind mine. I pulled out quickly, imagining for a moment what would happen if I had accidentally gone into reverse and slammed into them.

Back at the hotel, I cleaned up without cleaning up too much. I didn't want to hide my laptop and keys and stuff because I didn't want her to feel like I was hiding stuff but I also didn't want to leave too much out, just in case. So I took some of the money I had left in the room and some credit cards and hid them in the shoe in my suitcase and took out the condom and put it in my shaving case in the bathroom (much easier, if need be, to excuse

myself and go to the bathroom rather than excuse myself and rifle through my suitcase).

Then I watched a movie on HBO and fell asleep.

The next day, I checked out, grabbed breakfast at
McDonald's, and drove home.

Today I weigh 210 pounds.

DOUG 208 POUNDS

Jesus, I'm really late. Really really late. I wonder if she'll still be there. I wonder if she'll charge the girls extra. That would be fucking embarrassing, if I was the only one of the three of us who was late and they had to pay extra just for me. Like being the roommate who's responsible for losing the security deposit. I could offer to pay the charge, or whatever. Fuck that. Who is she to charge us extra? So I'm late. It's our time, it's paid for, if she's being paid to sit there alone and watch cable waiting for me so be it. Fucking bitch, you won't get another cent from us. Still, I feel bad. But it's not like I didn't have extraneous circumstances. Witness my shoes and my forehead. Shit, I'm fucking sweating. I don't want to be one of the fat fucking sweaty slobs she has to deal with every night. Difference being I'm not that fat anymore, yeah, wa-hoo. Maybe I could shower first. I could have her get into the shower with me. Have her shower while I take a little nap, that might be nice.

God my heart is pounding, how far away is this fucking place? "Sorry I'm late." Or why should I feel like I have to start from a position of weakness, like she's *my* superior? "Hey, I'm late." Just to acknowledge. "Let's get this over with." Probably best not to say that out loud. People don't say that to their dentist. "Let's get this the fuck over with, Dr. Morgenstern, you fucking fluoride-dealing whore." Is that as funny as I think it is? It's getting cold as fuck out here but I've sweated through this fucking shirt. Should've brought another shirt.

There wasn't anyone else around for miles is what's so weird about it. Fucking humiliating, if you want to know the truth. I guess I'm more rattled by all this than I thought I was. Who am I to get rattled? This is nothing. No big deal. I'm not nervous. I'm not anxious. This is just like one of those bachelor nights when it was slim pickings but I wanted to get with someone and didn't care who it was, just had to put a little more effort into it, not focus on her ass, blur my vision a little when I couldn't avoid looking at her face, then get the hell out of there as early as possible. This is just like one of those nights. Difference being that this girl is hot. And my wife paid for her. And the idea of getting inside her fills me with dread. And I just plowed my car into a telephone pole. Yeah, other than those things, this is no big fucking deal.

I thought. Losing weight meant. Not getting all. Out of. Breath.

I see the sign. The hotel. Almost there.

Man, it's getting cold already.

Don't want to tell Cheryl about this, the car. So stupid. She already thinks I'm enough of an idiot. Find some way to keep it from her. Probably shouldn't tell this chick about it either then, she's Brin's friend, it'll get around. And I sure as hell don't need Randy and Martin knowing about it. "What the hell, Doug, you were so rattled you got into a single-vehicle accident on the way there and just left your car and walked like fifty thousand miles to the hotel and got your shoes all wet? What the hell is up with that? She's just a prostitute, man." I wasn't rattled, you assholes, this is actually a function of my getting a hundred times more tail than either of you could ever hope to do, not that you'd understand that. So I'll keep it from them. This is what it's all come to, this is what this scheme has brought me, now I'm lying to my friends and to my wife. Well, I was already lying to my wife. But this is about new stuff, for Christ's sake.

I need to be a new person. A better person, seriously. I've had these thoughts before, after my dad died, after my doctor told me to get my cholesterol down, but I'm serious this time. Need to stop cheating on Cheryl, which apparently will be easy since other women have evidently lost all interest in me. Need to stop treating people like shit. I'm serious this time, the access road to this Marriott loading dock is my road to fucking Damascus, I'm going to be a complete and total saint. After I'm done banging this prostitute and lying about the car. Things are about to change. Big time.

Everyone in the lobby giving me looks. "Who's that sweaty, not-terribly-fat bastard?" Fuck off you fucks, have you never seen a john on his way to a trick before? Probably seen enough hookers walk through the door of this place. In at eleven. Out by midnight. Fuckin' concierge probably knows the local ladies of the eve by name. "Evenin', Betsy." Who the fuck ever heard of a hooker named Betsy? Focus, man. Focus. In the moment. In the moment. Be here. Now. Nowhere else. No past. No future. Right. Now.

Eleventh floor. Okay. Deep breaths. It's all good. I'm in charge.

"Sorry I'm late. I mean, hey, I'm late."

She's cute. Looks older than I expected. But hey, aren't we all.

"You're cute. Not that old. Aw Jesus, give me a second."

Why's she looking at me like that? Sweat is her stock in trade, if she were an ER nurse she wouldn't be repulsed by my blood. Oh, shit, I should probably explain my blood.

"Cut myself." She's just staring. "Here. Ow!!" I probably didn't need to touch it, she can see where I'm bleeding. "What, you've never cut your forehead before?"

Sit down. She's helping me off with my shoes. That's sweet. Suddenly I feel like I'm at fucking Foot Locker. "Ten and a half. Heh heh." Always got a chub when the Foot Locker ladies were at my service. Kneel and let me assess your assets. She shouldn't crouch there just staring at me like that, it's making my vision spin. "Let's get this over with." Oops. "I wasn't supposed to say that out loud. I'm just going to lie down a second. I'll try not to bleed on the things." That's a nice ceiling. "I'm not passing out, I'm just horizontal. I don't know if this is one of those things where you're supposed to keep me talking so I don't pass out and die . . . if it is, you're doing a piss-poor job. But I'll defer to your judgment. Are you talking to me? Ah, I couldn't tell exactly. If I do die, tell my wife something? Tell her I did you from behind? Thanks. Even if I don't die." Yeah, I'm never going to get an erection this way. Maybe if I think of, what's her name, plays tennis, oh never mind . . . maybe she could . . . no. I lost the side bet. I can't ask her to do that. Fuck the side bet. Fuck the . . . oh yeah, I'm supposed to fuck her. Seems impossible in the current situation, circumstances being what they are, but if anyone can do this I can, even with sweat and blood in my eyes, it's like Robert Redford at the end of *The Natural,* like Jimmy Stewart at the end of *Mr. Smith,* like Stallone at the end of all the *Rocky*s, steep odds aren't going to scare off this john, having orgasms is my thing. In fact I'm going to do her twice, hey, she's not wearing underwear, that makes things easier. And one two three we're done, boy that was fun, well worth the past year and a half of misery and however much of our joint savings account Cheryl depleted to get me here, now just give me a second and we'll do it again, "Just give me a second" I say out loud, she's a professional and knows "a second" is a figure of speech, uh-oh, ceiling receding, she's flying away, oh God, probably not supposed to lose consciousness, bad idea medically and also for this transaction number two here, but so sleepy, sleepy, sleepy, I'm the sleepiest bleedingest john in hookerville . . .

RANDY 206 POUNDS

In the beginning—and by beginning I mean the time between the expectedly awkward "hello" and the point where she said, "Hmmm. You're fun. Want to try something a little different?"—she was very, I don't know, professional. For a hooker, I mean. And I mean it in a good way. Professional, I mean. She explained that we had an hour to party and that there really wasn't a limit on what happened.

She wasn't really my type—I don't mean as a hooker, I mean as a civilian. As a person. As a woman. Put her in a room with five other hooker-type women . . . or any women for that matter . . . and she might be my third choice. Not that I'd end up in a room like that.

I'm not saying the hooker was unattractive. Not at all. Tight body. Welcoming face. Cute little mole right above her collarbone. Gorgeous, thick black hair. She talked to me as if I was a person and our conversation was a lot more natural than the one I had with the masseuse when Dierdre and I were on vacation. That woman was gorgeous and I could have sworn that when she left the room in the middle of doing my legs that she was going somewhere to vomit.

The hooker, though, never made me feel like she wanted to be anywhere but in the room with me. She wasn't saying stupid bad-actressy things. It wasn't like that. She was just being cool, like she was in a hotel room with me and she wanted to have some fun.

Fun.

That's what I had to remind myself. This is supposed to be fun. It's not love. It's like wasting an hour at a casino table. Or indulging in a mindless novel. Or watching an afternoon of junk TV. Or eating a bag of cheese curls. An entire bag of cheese curls. The kind where you have to wash your hands afterward.

There's not a moral issue here. There's a woman who wants to have fun and a man who wants to have fun and another woman who is cool with the whole idea. That woman is happy that the man and the other woman are having fun because that woman knows that the second woman isn't any sort of threat. She's no more of a threat than an hour at the casino table. Or a mindless novel. Or an afternoon of junk TV. Or that bag of cheese curls.

I'm done thinking about that when she undoes my belt. My new belt. The one I bought last week. The one that doesn't look like it could lasso a steer.

I don't forget Dierdre. She's just, while the clock is running, not vital to the equation. She's earlier and later. She's not right now. She'll be there when this is done. I know that. And I'll be there when this is done. I want that. But with my belt off and her unbuttoning her blouse and me wondering when the last time was when I unhooked a bra with one hand (long enough for the clasps to have changed. I used to be good at that) I'm able to compartmentalize this.

And when I'm inside her, it feels damn good. It feels like harmony.

It feels like I've got nothing to worry about.

It feels like there's a new discovery every second. A glimpse of the side of her neck or the feel of the space on the bottom of her forearm or the sound she makes when I try twisting my hips a little the way that Dierdre likes.

I don't care if she's a pro. Some things benefit from professionalism. I'm not going to go see an amateur football game. I don't want to see a community theater perform *Death of a Salesman*. I don't want my steak prepped by a kid from McDonald's. I do want my steak served with a baked potato stuffed with sour cream and bacon, but I don't want that prepped by the kid from McDonald's either.

Professionalism is good. Because she's a pro, I don't have to lie. I don't have to guess. I don't have to wonder what she's feeling (even though I can still try to make her feel good). I don't have to worry about what she's going to ask me or what she's going to tell me or if she knows someone I know or if she's going to hate me or what she's going to think of my abilities or the size of my stomach or the sound I make when I explode—which I almost do twice but manage to control because, hell, I've got time.

Then she says, "Hmmm. You're fun. Want to try something a little different?" and I kind of laugh and she kind of laughs and it's like playing poker when you have to make a really quick hold 'em or fold 'em decision and you know that in fifteen seconds you are either going to beat yourself up with regret or be in a whole new world you didn't even know existed. What I wanted, I guess, is for her to say, "Here, try this." To hell with *Jeopardy!*, I didn't want my hooker night phrased in the form of a question. I wanted a statement.

No, I wanted a command.

Instead: "Hmmm. You're fun. Want to try something a little different?"

DOUG 210 POUNDS

I wish Randy didn't tell me when he'd be with her. Bastard.

Maybe get on the treadmill for a little while.

Maybe watch some TV.

Maybe call my brother, who I haven't spoken to since Christmas. I think I missed one of his kid's birthdays. I know Cheryl sent them something for Christmas, but I'm not sure about their birthdays.

Her legs are open and Randy is pumping away, sweating away. I hope she's looking at her watch like in, shit, what movie was it where the hooker was looking at her watch?

Randy's finally losing his innocence. Me, I lost a lot of blood. Need evidence that this world's being administrated by a fucked-up unjust god, look no further.

Maybe finally clean those leaves out of the gutter.

Maybe update my résumé.

Maybe click on some porn.

Maybe heat up some of the leftover fajitas.

Maybe see if it's time yet to pop another pain pill.

Maybe see if Cheryl wants to have a go. Or at least if she's speaking to me again. She's acting like she bought me a new expensive silk tie and I got something on it the first time I wore it. Is it my fault I drove off the road? Technically, yes, I know, it is. But she should pity me, shouldn't she? I was promised fun, I got an ER visit and fucked-up front-end suspension. Pity me! Of course, she thinks I got the fun along with the ER visit.

Maybe she hates herself for getting me a hooker and she's taking it out on me.

Maybe sending me off to sleep with this other woman made her realize about all the other times.

Maybe she gets that she hasn't wanted to be married to me for a long time.

Maybe my life's finally falling apart.

Maybe I should see about that pain pill.

RANDY 206 POUNDS

And we did something a little different—in some ways, a lot different—from what I've done with Dierdre. And within about three minutes, I was done. Totally done. And the feeling was different, especially right afterward, when I'm used to my head spinning like I just got pushed off the merry-go-round and I'm not sure what part of the universe I landed in. Like the void where the intensity of the buildup was suddenly filled with whatever random shit my subconscious could pour into it.

And it wasn't just the act that was done, it was something else that was done. I slid out and tried to focus my mind and reached around her to hold her for a second and I held on tight, around her ribs and I slid my hand down to let her know that I would try my best to take her somewhere if she wanted to go there and she knew what I was trying to do and, I think, like me, she didn't know if I was doing it out of some effort to be a gentleman or if I was doing it because I enjoyed the feeling of taking her somewhere near where I had just been. And, like me, she probably knew that there wasn't a big difference between the two.

So what did I just do?

And who am I?

MARTIN 209 POUNDS

We went out to dinner. Went to a movie. Stopped for ice cream afterward (one scoop, no mix-in). Didn't say a word about what's happening in a few days. Who am I kidding: three days. A couple of times during the night, whenever there was a longish pause in the conversation, I tried to guess what she was going to say. Or what topic she was going to hit when we started talking again. The kids. Something she read in a magazine. A question about work. I guessed right two out of eight times, which I'm not sure is good or bad. Since it's a new game, there are no statistics to compare it to.

But it seems that two out of eight is pretty good.

RANDY 205 POUNDS

"Bless me father, for I have . . . I think . . . sinned. It has been two and a half years since my last confession and I bet you haven't heard this one before."

MARTIN 208 POUNDS

I killed a half hour in the bookstore during lunch looking at books on sexual positions. There were a surprising number of these books, making me wonder if I'll ever let the kids wander around a bookstore ever again.

In the book that seemed the most authoritarian and yet had the most pictures (I didn't have *that* much time), I counted seven positions that I tried with Amy and nine with Brin, five of them overlapping. Don't know how that puts me statistically with the rest of the free world, but that's not really the issue. The issue—or, rather, the question—is, do I go with what I know or take this as an opportunity to experiment?

DOUG 212 POUNDS

It's first thing in the morning and we're sitting in the kitchen doing our first-thing-in-the-morning stuff and I just look over at her and go, "You never thought we would make it, did you?"

She looks at me, all blank.

"The three of you, your whole plan was predicated on none of us ever making it down to 210 pounds. You never planned on having to hire Brin's friend. The entire scheme hung on this smug, superior conviction that you knew everything, that you were in control, that we were a bunch of hapless boobs who would never get it together, we'd lose enough weight to look better but not enough to win the bet and you'd go through the rest of life being the smart one. Right about now you're all kicking yourselves that you didn't say 190 pounds."

She doesn't say anything.

"If I didn't know you better," I say, "I'd guess that there was never a prostitute in the picture until you realized you had no other choice."

Then her eyes harden, and she gets up and leaves the kitchen.

Maybe I went too far, suggesting she'd do something stupid like that. But I was just making a point.

My head throbs.

BRIN

Are you going to wear that shirt?

I'm not saying anything. I'm just asking, "Are you going to wear that shirt?"

I don't mean anything by it.

Fine.

I'm just saying, if it were me, I wouldn't wear that shirt. It's not terribly attractive, is all. I know you don't need to be terribly attractive on this particular evening, I'm just saying I don't know why one would deliberately choose to be not terribly attractive, especially after one has lost all this weight and is generally looking pretty good. Unless that's the point, unless you enjoy the prospect of wearing something that's actually mildly hideous and still getting lucky at the end of the evening in spite of it. Unless that's some kind of a kick, which I guess I can see why it might be, intellectually. I can intellectualize why it might be kind of a kick. It's just always been a little bit of a horrible shirt, is all I'm saying, and I know she won't like it. Well, I know she won't. I just know. I know her, right? We've known each other for years, known each other since college supposedly, so I know what she likes and I know she won't like that. That's all. All I'm saying.

Oh, are you changing your shirt?

Whatever you want.

Sorry? When I said what? I said "supposedly"? I don't know why. I didn't mean anything by it, certainly. It didn't mean anything, we've known each other since college, period. It's just one of those words that don't mean anything anymore, that people just say to up their daily word count, like "literally" or "actually." Supposedly. You know, 40 percent of all the words we say don't mean a single thing anyway. Literally.

You going to wear those shoes? I'm just asking.

You what? Well, you shouldn't. Seriously, you shouldn't feel bad. That's another one of those words: "seriously." Only in this case I mean it: seriously, you shouldn't feel bad. Why should you feel bad? This was my idea, I pushed you into it, the only reason people feel bad in situations like this is because they're betraying the other person, and I'm the other person, and it was all my idea, so you shouldn't feel bad. Seriously. I'm approving. I'm sitting here. I'm helping you with your shirt choices. There's no reason to feel bad. Unless you're feeling bad about exploiting another woman's body for money or participating in an inherently unequal misogynistic institution. But you shouldn't feel bad on my account, or your account, we're all happy, we're all good. See, happy? I don't look happy? How about now? Now? How about now? Oh, screw it, I'm happy, all right, take my word for it, I'm happy. This can't hurt anything if we don't let it hurt anything. Let's you and I make a date for a roll in the hay on Tuesday—I figure you might be a little sore and that will give you time to recover. You can tell me about it or not tell me about it then. It'll probably really, you know, get me going. Seriously. If nothing else, do it for us. For the romp we're going to have on Tuesday.

Those pants look good. I knew they'd look good. She won't know they're from Target.

What? No, there's no need. See, we're both in this together, so we don't need to achieve parity, we're already, what's the word, we're already at par. This isn't some Updike novel, nobody's keeping track on some moral balance sheet, we're balanced. I don't need any consideration. "Consideration," where'd you get that word?

What?

One more time?

Well, I don't know. I guess I just don't know, Martin. Hmm, let me think. Does he have to be one of your friends? I've seen most of your friends, Martin, you'd have to do better than that.

And for everything to come out equal, what, I'd need to do something, right? Earn it somehow. Like you with the weight. You think I need to lose weight, Martin? Is that what you're getting at? No, I know I need to lose some weight, I'm asking whether you think I need to lose some weight. My butt's too big for you, is it? I get a smaller butt, I can sleep with some young stud, is that it? Then what? Why are you getting so flustered? I'm just asking. What would I have to do? What would make you happy? Okay, not happy, what would make me better? How about a boob job, that sound good? Go up a couple sizes? Some liposuction, some Botox, how about a total extreme makeover? Martin? Is that what you're saying? Let's just lay our cards on the table. Martin? Martin.

MARTIN 209 POUNDS

Well, that was a mistake, to bring that up.

I thought I was being nice, reciprocal. Like if she gets me a gift, I get her a gift. She gets me a watch, I get her a sweater. Or vice versa. No, really what I thought I was doing was idle speculation, talking to fill the time and to fill my mind, because I was getting ready for this date with a stranger and Brin was sitting on the bed and if she said one more word about my shirt or my pants I thought I would lose my mind.

Still, seemed harmless. Who knew? This thing I'm doing, that was her idea, was allegedly a loving and generous and selfless thing when she offered it to me, is a piggish and shallow and insensitive thing when I offer it to her. I guess context really is everything. Still, I'm a little floored. Can't believe I didn't see it coming. I felt so clueless, so self-absorbed, so freaking male. I felt like Doug, for God's sake. Usually I'm okay at stuff like that. Seeing her side. Being attentive and sensitive. I hate those lousy comedians who think it's eternally fresh and funny to anatomize the ways in which men and women are different from each other. Tim Allen. Elayne Boosler. Men like *SportsCenter*, women like *The View*. Ho ho. Men don't ask for directions. It is very comical. Men like tools. Women like to cuddle. Men can't say anything right. Women will turn on you and tear you a new one at the least provocation. Men are idiots. Women are dangerous. Men hide. Women kill. Men are dogs. Women are cats. I realized I was standing in my bedroom in my socks just like Tim Allen. God, that's a fate fit for no man.

And she knew it, I think. Saw what I hated about myself at that moment and targeted it. "Boob job," indeed. She knows I don't want her to get a boob job. She knows I'm more into her legs anyway. Is there such a thing as a leg job? Best not to ask.

Standing in my bedroom with my pants unzipped like Doug. God, what's become of me? Why can't I look forward to this thing the way Doug no doubt did? It's not me. Can't do it. I don't laugh at jokes about how much men hate shopping, and I can't wait for this evening of wild ecstasy to be over.

RANDY 206 POUNDS

The girl in the picture didn't have a mole on her collar-bone.

MARTIN 208 POUNDS

If I were a stand-up comedian I'd do a bit about how I've eaten at International House of Pancakes maybe ten times and I've never had pancakes there. This is one of several dozen reasons why I'm not a stand-up comedian and why, instead, I'm a guy sitting at an International House of Pancakes at one thirty in the morning having the French toast. No syrup. Lots of butter. My thing.

You have to have "things." Everything else fades away. My great grandmother used to smoke skinny cigarettes. That was her thing. It's the only thing me and my cousins remember about her.

I don't know what my thing is. Certainly the "butter/no syrup" thing won't be passed from generation to generation. Maybe some people don't have a thing. It would be just like me to be one of those people.

The French toast came out cold. There's only three other people here. How can they not serve it hot? But I didn't want to make a scene. Historians, if there were historians who wrote about guys being fixed up with hookers by their wives, would note that I had a raw deal going in. I know it's not like we were all going right in a row, all in the same night, like the fellas in a teenage sex comedy from the '80s, where if you're the sixth of six to go sorry to say you're actually getting a lot more intimate with your buddies than with the girl. I know it wasn't like that.

But going last does sort of make you think about hygiene issues. I'm not preoccupied with hygiene issues, as long as I don't have to think about them. I know guys at work who won't even touch the bedspread in a hotel room but I won't even think about it as long as I didn't just see a local news report where they burst into a hotel room and used infrared technology to show how the whole place is a $110-a-night petri dish.

So there was that—the hygiene thing. Which is just one of the reasons why I didn't talk to Randy or Doug right after their evenings. Still haven't talked with them, in fact. I'm sure they had lovely times.

And there was the battle with Brin. Minor skirmish, really. Still, who does that? Who causes a fight with his wife before leaving to spend the night with the prostitute she paid for? Most fights end with me buying flowers. But this particular bundle would have to have three or four different notes attached. The most manic-depressive bouquet of flowers ever.

I'll ask the nice lady at the florist's. What do you give that says "the fight was my fault" and "thank you for the nice whore"?

"Was she a particularly good prostitute, sir? If so, I'd recommend some baby's breath."

Why do I suddenly, inappropriately, feel like Neil Armstrong?

Only not Neil Armstrong—whoever the third guy was to get out of the thing and walk around. Same idea.

My thing is, I can't stop thinking about my situation in terms of the situation. The weirdness of its generality is keeping me from engaging its specificity. I don't know what to do because I can't figure out what a guy in this situation should do. If I could stop worrying about the latter I'd probably be able to figure out the former. Had the same issue in the hotel room. First I was surprised that she was so normal. Just a person. Nice, attractive person I might have met anywhere. Kinko's. Home Depot. White Castle, if I went there anymore. IHOP. Pretty smile. Hugged me hello, which seemed weird, but I guess a handshake would have been weirder. Get the intimacy engine running early, time is money, plus get the guy comfortable. See, I couldn't lose sight of me as "the guy."

She made conversation. Actually had some pretty funny things to say, about the hotel and the minibar and people she saw on the elevator. She talked about Brin, their college days, which seemed calculated and weirdly distant and also quite ill-advised, I thought. "Yeah, we just had a fight," I said. Awkward silence. Even more ill-advised. That's not the sort of thing the guy's supposed to say. I'm guessing. First, she's Brin's friend. Second, Brin's her client. Third, they're partners in the global sisterhood. If I say Brin and I had a fight and this woman takes my side, I'll know she's only doing it because of the money, yet another distasteful thing she's doing because of the money, and I'll feel like a kid who has to pay a classmate a dollar to be his friend. Not that I ever did that. Someone else paid me once, actually, a total loser in second grade named Kimball paid me a dollar and within a week I gave him a full refund. It seriously just wasn't worth it.

I was a bad person as a second grader, wasn't I?

Bringing it home there in that hotel bed was supposed to feel like crossing a finish line, I think: my great reward, a fabulous prize, the end of a great adventure. Finally arriving in Canterbury, the party with the Ewoks, drinking with the other hobbits back in the shire, graduating from freaking Hogwarts.

Instead, well, instead I told her that I'm sure there are lots of guys who just want to talk. She said, "yes." I told her I wasn't one of them. Because I didn't really want to talk. What I wanted was some French toast, from IHOP. She said it would be her treat.

So I didn't bring it home in that hotel bed. Instead, now, I'm having a late-night breakfast with a woman who probably slept with a half-dozen guys today and she borrowed a pencil from the waitress and is doing the crossword puzzle in the local paper after having stashed the placemat with its puzzles and mazes in her purse for her youngest son. And I'm looking at her. And she knows it.

Mostly we sit in comfortable silence. Comfortable silence with a woman is actually something worth paying for; apart from Brin and Amy it's been tough to come by. But occasionally we talk. Sometimes she says things I don't fully understand, like when she says "Now this, this is pretty different." Whatever that means. But also we talk about our kids, about the idiot parents at our kids' schools. Her kids go to private school so we talk about the uniforms. All the time we talk waiting for our breakfasts she's doing this puzzle.

Then she says, "I need a seven-letter word for renaissance."

And I'm thinking about painting and sculpting and inventing flying machines before I realize what she's asking for. "Rebirth."

RANDY 206 POUNDS

Reasons this whole thing was kind of a cool thing, considering:

1. I think she really liked me. The way you can sometimes tell the difference between a waitress who likes you for the tip and the one who likes you regardless? I think I could tell. She really liked me. And that feels kind of good. Obviously. Because, you know, little fish, big pond. I think she's got a really, really big pond.

2. I look a lot better. And you figure I must be a lot healthier. Apart from the heart attack, I mean.

3. Dierdre seems happier than she's, like, ever been.

4. My sexual parameters have been totally made way bigger. Which I didn't even think I wanted. But I guess that's how it is, with parameters.

Reasons this whole thing has been kind of weird:

1. I haven't talked to Martin or Doug, or e-mailed them or anything, for a while. Since, in fact. When was the last time that happened? I don't know because we don't keep track the way I think girls do, with their mental, whatever, spreadsheets or Palm Pilots, whatever they've got in their heads that keeps track of who wrote

who last and who asks who out to lunch and stuff like that. But still, it's some kind of a first. And another thing:

2. I don't really even miss them. What's that about?

3. Dierdre seems happier than she's, like, ever been.

4. I had a heart attack. I've stared death in the face or whatever and yet I feel nothing like Anthony Hopkins in that Brad Pitt movie. I feel more like Brad Pitt in that *Thelma and Louise* movie, only without the stealing and the being a bad guy.

5. Dierdre made me tell her everything that happened. She was waiting for me when I got home, which didn't surprise me, I sort of expected it I think, either because she'd want to make sure my heart was okay or because she wanted to look me in the face and see if I'd changed or how much I liked it. But it wasn't either of those things, she wanted me to tell her everything and wanted to ask me right away so I wouldn't forget anything. (Like I'd forget anything!) As I went through it all she looked at me with a look you don't see on Dierdre very often, a look like she's looking at one of those magic eye 3-D posters and trying to make it go 3-D. Real serious-looking, not even blinking. When I was done she goes "Thanks" and leaves, like she's going to write it all down. (I wonder if she went to write it all down?)

6. I can tell she's, Cinnamon's, not the girl in the picture, and I haven't said anything. It seems all sort of minor at this point, don't you think?

6a. Her name's Cinnamon, by the way, it turns out, which I think counts as kind of weird.

7. We're seeing her again this weekend. Together. The three of us, me and Dierdre and Cinnamon, together. Uncharted territory. Exploration time. Hell, what's the harm? Dierdre's idea actually. She's into it. I'm into it. Cinnamon's, well, like I said: I think she liked me. Plus, we've set aside money in the household budget for it.

To: Mr. Doug E. Garrison, Jr., esquire, incorporated
From: Mrs. Cheryl Everett Garrison, wife, flesh of your &c. &c.
Re: The end of the world as we know it

WHEREAS the party of the first part (hereinafter known as "Doug") dutifully engaged in a harebrained scheme at the insistence of the party of the second part (hereinafter referred to as "Cheryl"), and

WHEREAS said harebrained scheme was designed to make everything about our lives better, e.g., health, happiness, increased mutual desire and decreased mutual loathing, and

WHEREAS said harebrained scheme seemed at first to be working at least with regard to health insofar as you no longer cause a worldwide rayon shortage every time you go pants shopping and smartass kids across the mall parking lot no longer call out "Hey look, it's Jimmy Kimmel! Hey, Jimmy Kimmel!" when they see you, but

WHEREAS you probably don't have to be Dr. Joyce Brothers to realize that enforced infidelity probably isn't the best way to strengthen a marriage and that it's likely to have all sorts of deep-seated not-entirely-unforeseen effects sprinkled in its wake like so many land mines, and

WHEREAS I've actually been lying to you a lot in the past few months, which makes me feel like shit but which has also had the peculiar and elusive and not at all provable effect of making me review your behavior over the course of our marriage and realize in retrospect that I think you've probably lied to me more than I thought you did, and

WHEREAS our marriage might have limped through its last forty years or so perfectly amiably and undisturbed if we'd never embarked on the aforementioned harebrained scheme but something about the unfamiliarity of the whole experience threw what we have into a new relief and made one or (I hope) both parties realize that we haven't had anything really in common for quite a long time, and

WHEREAS I know it would be lame, unfair, and totally uncool for the party of the second part to blame the party of the first part for sleeping with another woman when it was entirely the party of the second part's idea, but

WHEREAS I blame you for sleeping with that other woman, then

THEREFORE let it be known that I'm pretty sure our marriage is over, and

FURTHERMORE that you can have the house and stuff, I just need to get out of here and feeling like I'd made anything like a profit off this whole thing would freak me out for reasons you'd never understand, and

MOREOVER let it be known that the only way I could tell you this was in writing, and the only way I could write it is by trying to be funny, because anything else and I'm pretty sure I would dissolve.

This so-and-so date of &c., &c.,

C.

To: MBB@yahoo.com, Randy 12479@aol.com
From: Doug@freemail.com
Subject: Sup?

Hey guys, what's up? Want to get together and hang out sometime? (I ask with the pretense of not knowing the answer as a courtesy because what are the chances two lame assholes like your fine selves would have other social plans?) I need a break from the whole finding-a-job-selling-the-house shit which is kicking my ass.

@@@Get a free e-mail account from freemail TODAY!@@@

To: Doug@freemail.com, Randy 12479@aol.com
From: MBB@yahoo.com
Subject: Re: Sup?

Sure, yeah, that would be fun, sometime. We should figure out a time, sometime. Or something. Good to hear from you.

To: Doug@freemail.com, MBB@yahoo.com
From: Randy 12479@aol.com
Subject: Two pounds

Sure that would be fine. My weekends are crazy though, probably be a while before they settle down. We should do that though.

Randy

"Winning begets winning."

Dear Mr. Westfeldt,

I've long been an admirer of the television films you've produced. Okay, that's a lie. You have, after all, primarily produced films for a cable network that calls itself "television for women," and I am not, truth be told, a woman. I've seen quite a bit of your work, however, inadvertently and otherwise, largely on weekends on laundry days when I was married, and I'm impressed with the scope and volume of your output. I'm aware as well, after some Internet research, that you seem to specialize in films based on real-life stories. This is why I am contacting you on this occasion: I have a real-life story I think could be a candidate for film adaptation. It incorporates many of the American television viewing audience's chief obsessions, most notably sex and weight loss.

I would welcome discussing the project with you in more detail. My only concerns are that the story, properly told, would involve a lot of actual sex as well as profanity, so maybe it would do better as a theatrical release. But you know more about such things than I do. I'm also interested in knowing whether it's customary in such situations for the hatcher of the idea to get paid up front, and if so, how much.

I think it could make for a very successful movie,

albeit with a few requisite changes. The ending, for one thing, should be happy.

I can be reached at the phone number above. I look forward to speaking with you.

Sincerely,
Doug E. Garrison

Randy,

I think this is a GREAT start. Really SUPER. But as you get into it remember the things we discussed:

1. Focus!!!
2. NO LISTS!!

I also wonder about whether this is the best magazine to send it to first, or are there higher-class ones to start with? *The New Yorker* probably doesn't take stuff like this, huh? But I always enjoy it in the dentist's office, so worth checking.

Cinnamon and I will see you after work tonight, rrowwr!!

Love, D.

>>

>>Dear Penthouse Forum,

I never thought anything like this would ever happen to me. It all began when my wife said she'd like me to lose some weight, and wanted to offer me an incentive to do so. This plan led, over the course of some months, to the following developments:

1. A friend's old college friend, now a high-priced prostitute
2. New toys and tools I'd never encountered before
3. Lots of threesomes

Also a heart attack, but I'm not going to talk about that here. Or the stuff going on with my friends, who can sometimes be jerks.

MARTIN 208 POUNDS

You are what you do, I guess.

I mean, I could think all day about helping the homeless or visiting the sick or whatever, but if I don't do it, then I didn't do it. Then I'm not the kind of guy who would do that.

So I lost a lot of weight. I'm a guy who lost a lot of weight.

I used to be the kind of guy who couldn't do that. Now I'm the kind of guy who can. Who did. What does that make me?

A thinner guy.

Whose wife loved him so much that she did something pretty outrageous to make sure that he'd drop some serious pounds.

Also, the kind of guy who has only given half of himself to his wife because he's still got a thing for his first wife. Had a thing. Got a thing. I don't know.

But that doesn't matter. That's the stuff in my head.

There's a lot of stuff in there.

Like this: I'm not sure if what I was going to do with the hooker would be as bad as what I didn't do with that stripper I tried to get to my room on that business trip.

Yes, that was nothing worse than a lap dance. But I did open a door into my marriage with Amy. Doesn't matter what Amy was doing at the time. If she was doing anything, I didn't know about it. So it doesn't matter what she did. What matters is what *I've* done. Or would have done.

For all intents and purposes, I cheated on Amy. I didn't cheat on Brin, no matter what would have happened with the hooker. But I did cheat on Amy.

What else?

Well, I've lost a boatload of weight.

And I'm going to keep it off. Maybe even see the south side of 200.

And I've committed to Brin. Even if we're going to fight. Even if we're going to get frustrated with each other. Even if the annoyances come closer and closer together. And even if my mind sometimes goes to Amy, so be it. Nobody's got to know.

Same with the hooker.

Same with the stripper.

Same with Marie Osmond, for that matter.

There's no reason that Brin's got to know when my mind drifts to the way the hooker would have slid her hips at just the right time or the way her hair would have fallen down across the pillow. Or about how Amy looked on our wedding night.

But even that memory is fading. Maybe not fading. Archived is more like it. Archived in the museum of my brain. The hooker file and the Amy file. I have access. They're part of the permanent collection. They are a part of me. A place for my mind to go when my mind needs to go there.

But Brin isn't in the archives.

Brin is here.

Brin married me, the fat me, because she had some kind of faith in me. And I never took a condom on a business trip while I was married to Brin. That has to mean something.

And when I came home from being with the hooker, all I wanted to do was make love with Brin. That has to mean something too.

I think I won this thing. Hand me a trophy. No speeches.

ROBERT DE NIRO 228 POUNDS

Dear Randy Tonelli,

    Thank you for writing. I always appreciate hearing from my fans. An autographed photograph is enclosed. Thank you again.

Robert De Niro

ABOUT THE AUTHORS

LOU HARRY'S books include *Creative Block: 500 Ideas to Ignite the Imagination*, *The Encyclopedia of Guilty Pleasures*, and others. He lives with his wife and four kids in Indianapolis, where he edits *Indy Men's Magazine*. Write him at workforlou@aol.com. Ask him to your book group's meeting. Especially if you are serving pizza.

ERIC PFEFFINGER is an award-winning playwright whose plays, including *Accidental Rapture* and *Mouse Cop*, have been produced in Chicago, L.A., Off-Off-Broadway, and elsewhere. A contributor to National Lampoon.com and various magazines, he lives in Toledo, Ohio.